W9-AND-092

*In which Ashleigh discovers Jane Austen,
and her wardrobe, to the embarrassment of Julie.*

"Listen, Ash," I said. "You're not planning to go to school wearing that, are you? No guy will even *look* at you." Me neither if they see me with you, I added inwardly. "Couldn't you please, please, please wear jeans?"

As always, my plea fell on deaf ears.

"I see not the necessity of discussing with *you*, Miss Lefkowitz, the propriety of a young lady wearing Trousers. As you know, modesty forbids us to reveal the shape of the Lower Limbs."

"If you do get a boyfriend, he's going to want to see a lot more than just the shape of your Lower Limbs," I argued.

Fortunately, I reflected, the school year wouldn't start for another week—enough time, I hoped, to make her see reason.

✑

OTHER BOOKS YOU MAY ENJOY

Enthusiasm
Polly Shulman

speak
An Imprint of Penguin Group (USA) Inc.

SPEAK
Published by the Penguin Group
Penguin Group (USA) Inc., 345 Hudson Street, New York, New York 10014, U.S.A.
Penguin Group (Canada), 90 Eglinton Avenue East, Suite 700, Toronto, Ontario, Canada M4P 2Y3
(a division of Pearson Penguin Canada Inc.)
Penguin Books Ltd, 80 Strand, London WC2R 0RL, England
Penguin Ireland, 25 St Stephen's Green, Dublin 2, Ireland (a division of Penguin Books Ltd)
Penguin Group (Australia), 250 Camberwell Road, Camberwell, Victoria 3124, Australia
(a division of Pearson Australia Group Pty Ltd.)
Penguin Books India Pvt Ltd, 11 Community Centre,
Panchsheel Park, New Delhi - 110 017, India
Penguin Group (NZ), 67 Apollo Drive, Rosedale, North Shore 0745, Auckland, New Zealand
(a division of Pearson New Zealand Ltd.)
Penguin Books (South Africa) (Pty) Ltd, 24 Sturdee Avenue,
Rosebank, Johannesburg 2196, South Africa

Registered Offices: Penguin Books Ltd, 80 Strand, London WC2R 0RL, England

First published in the United States of America by G. P. Putnam's Sons,
a division of Penguin Young Readers Group, 2006
Published by Speak, an imprint of Penguin Group (USA) Inc., 2007

1 3 5 7 9 10 8 6 4 2

Copyright © Polly Shulman, 2006
All rights reserved

THE LIBRARY OF CONGRESS HAS CATALOGED THE G. P. PUTNAM'S SONS EDITION AS FOLLOWS:
Shulman, Polly. Enthusiasm / Polly Shulman.   p.   cm.
Summary: Julie and Ashleigh, high school sophomores and Jane Austen fans,
seem to fall for the same Mr. Darcy–like boy and struggle to hide their true feelings
from one another while rehearsing for a school musical.
ISBN 0-399-24389-5(hc)
[1. Interpersonal relations—Fiction. 2. Musicals—Fiction. 3. Schools—Fiction.]
I. Title. PZ7.S55949Ent 2006   [Fic]—dc22   2005013490

Speak ISBN 978-0-14-240935-0

Printed in the United States of America

Design by Gunta Alexander
Text set in Aldus

Except in the United States of America, this book is sold subject to the condition that
it shall not, by way of trade or otherwise, be lent, re-sold, hired out, or otherwise
circulated without the publisher's prior consent in any form of binding or cover
other than that in which it is published and without a similar condition
including this condition being imposed on the subsequent purchaser.

The publisher does not have any control over and does not assume
any responsibility for author or third-party Web sites or their content.

For Anna Christina and Andrew

Chapter 1

There is little more likely to exasperate a person of sense than finding herself tied by affection and habit to an Enthusiast. I speak from bitter experience. My best friend and next-door neighbor, Ashleigh Marie Rossi, is an Enthusiast.

All last summer, Ashleigh was mad for the Wet Blankets. On the day they released their new album, she insisted that I accompany her to Outer Music, where they had advertised free tickets for a Blankets concert in the city. We started at ten o'clock in the morning, the break of dawn, Ashleigh time. "Ash," I objected, "they said they won't give out tickets till midnight. What are we going to do for fourteen hours?"

"You don't want to be stuck at the end of the line, do you? Don't worry, I packed lunch. Here, take one of these," she said, hauling a large woolen blanket out of her closet and dumping it in my arms.

"What's this for? It's about a million degrees out there. We'll be sitting in the sun."

"That's why we're bringing these!" She flourished two five-liter bottles of mineral water. "Wet Blankets, get it? We'll be appropriately dressed, and they'll keep us cool through the process of evaporation." She opened one of the bottles and reached out to splash me with the water.

"Ash, you freak, get away! Stop it! I'm not sitting around in the middle of town with my clothes soaked!"

With difficulty, I persuaded her to recap the water bottle, but nothing would convince her to leave the blankets behind. At Outer Music, we spread them on the sidewalk and sat down to wait. People looked at us strangely as they went in and out of the store, and I hid my face in my book, Jane Austen's *Pride and Prejudice*. At six o'clock, just as I reached the exciting proposal scene, Ashleigh's dad arrived with sandwiches. At nine, other Wet Blankets fans began lining up behind us.

Ashleigh's blankets came in handy after all, when the skies opened in a cloudburst around eleven. Overjoyed to find that Fate had cooperated with her planned pun, she invited her co-fans to seek shelter with us under the blankets.

This sort of behavior was nothing new for Ashleigh. All through elementary school, her crazes kept me in a constant flame of embarrassment. After she read the Little House books, it was all I could do to stop her from wearing her flowered flannel nightgown to the mall. During her Harriet-the-Spy period, which coincided with my parents' breakup when we were eleven, I had to confiscate two of her notebooks to keep them from falling into the hands of the divorce lawyers. When King Arthur ruled supreme in her heart, she thee'd and thou'd everyone from teachers to bus drivers.

But although our classmates considered Ashleigh weird back then, they respected her for her courage and inventiveness. Nothing ever embarrassed Ashleigh. Teasing her was pointless, since nobody could make her cry. Some of her reputation for oddness rubbed off on me, but so did some of her oddball prestige. Hanging out with Ashleigh in elementary school stopped just short of social suicide.

High school, though, was another matter. By then her ability to ignore giggles and stares had become less an asset than a liability. Oh, we still had plenty of friends—girls like Emily Mehan and the Gerard twins—but if Ash pulled any more stunts like that time freshman year when she borrowed Michelle Jeffries's handbag for a juggling trick and spilled the contents, including a selection of feminine hygiene products, I feared for our social standing among the girls. And as for guys—well, *that* was too painful to bear thinking about.

One hot afternoon about a month after the Wet Blankets incident, I sat by my window peeling my sunburn and considering the coming school year. Although Ashleigh did tend to get carried away, the Wet Blankets was a perfectly respectable interest for a Byzantium High sophomore. If only it would last through the vital first few weeks of school! Could I possibly be so lucky?

Evidently not. A rap on my windowpane interrupted me in the middle of removing a satisfyingly large patch of skin. Looking up, I saw the Enthusiast herself perched outside my window. (For reasons of convenience and privacy, Ashleigh and I exchange visits by way of the oak tree whose branches graze both our bedroom windows, rather than by the doors.) She was wearing a long black garment that caught on the twigs; I recognized it as a robe from last year's Freshman Chorus.

"Miss Lefkowitz! Miss Lefkowitz! My dear Miss Lefkowitz," she called.

I hauled the window open wide. "What's all the 'Miss' stuff?" I said. "You're not starting on an etiquette craze, are you?"

Ashleigh shot me her second-favorite expression, Reproach Tinged with Disgust. (Her favorite is the Mad Gleam.) "Etiquette?" she cried. "I hope I always conduct myself as befits a young lady. But my dear Miss Lefkowitz, why did you wait so long before introducing me to the joys of Miss Austen's work? Elizabeth Bennet! Jane Bennet! The incomparable Mr. Darcy!" She waved my copy of *Pride and Prejudice* at me, dislodging baby acorns and a leaf or two.

My heart sank. How many weeks of antiquated grammar were we in for now? And it was my own fault too. While Ashleigh bounced around the room, knocking things over with her skirts and raving about Austen's heroines and the gentlemen they loved, I considered my situation. Always before, Ashleigh had started a craze, and I had followed. Now, for the first time, I had taken the lead, introducing her to an interest of my own. But how long would it be before her passion overshadowed mine? Would she take over my favorite books, leaving nothing for me? I was convinced that I felt as strongly about Jane Austen's books as Ashleigh had ever felt about any of her crazes, but my love was deep and silent—and therefore easily overshadowed. I would never, for example, speak Jane Austen's language. That would be undignified and unworthy of the writer I adored.

Rescuing my clock radio, which had tumbled off my nightstand and was hanging by its cord, I told myself sternly not to be so ungenerous. Ashleigh never hesitated to share *her* interests with *me*. If only! No, she always insisted on dragging me in, however boring or unpleasant I might find them. (Military strategy? Ballet? Ig, no thanks!—Although I did rather enjoy candy making and reptiles.) The only time Ash let me wiggle out of a craze was when she knew I couldn't afford it—and when that happened, she gave it up herself, generous girl that she was. She squelched a growing passion for horses, for example, because my mother couldn't pay for riding lessons after my parents' divorce. And Ashleigh's generosity didn't stop there. Whenever her crazes got me in trouble—like the time I ruined my father's barbecue tools digging military trenches in the lawn—she devoted her savings and countless Saturdays to repairing the damage.

As I contemplated my pettiness, Ashleigh startled me with an emphatic bounce. (She's always bouncing with excitement, and when she bounces, she *bounces*—particularly in the past year or so. For my part, I barely jiggle, no matter how vigorously I move.)

"And I believe I know where to find them!" she cried.

"Where to find what?" I asked.

Ashleigh gave me her you're-not-listening look, a variant on the ever popular Disgusted Reproach.

"Not what—who. Our heroes. What good is a heroine without a hero? From what I remember of freshman year, we will be hard-pressed to find even a single gallant at Byzantium High. I despair of finding a pair of them there! But fortunately, I have discovered the answer."

Clearly Ashleigh had finished the research portion of her fad and moved on to the active stage. Now that she had decided to enact a 200-year-old love story with us as the heroines, I was afraid the results would be mortifying.

Without much hope, I tried to head her off. "I thought you despised boy-crazy girls like Michelle Jeffries and those people. You always said crushes were for noodleheads."

Ashleigh drew herself up to her full height, which I couldn't have done in her position—standing on my bed—since my head would have hit the sloping roof; her figure may be more mature than mine, but she's six inches shorter.

"I speak not of crushes, Miss Lefkowitz," she replied, "but of True Love."

True Love! What girl hasn't dreamed of *that*? Even the shyest among us longs for a soul mate—someone who will understand our hopes and fears, laugh at our jokes, offer us his coat when the afternoon turns cold, charm our parents, and admire us, flaws and all (such as a sharp chin, perhaps, and a marked lack of jiggle).

Although I had never discussed it with anyone, not even Ashleigh, I shared that dream. My ideal hero borrowed his appearance from a guy I thought of as the Mysterious Stranger. I had seen him just five times. The first was by the swimming hole on a windy Saturday in late spring. A woman's hat blew off her head and flew straight for the water, when the stranger snatched a fallen branch from the ground and, with a daring leap, caught it. I had seen him twice since then in the state park, on foot and on horseback. Once I glimpsed him through the window of the Java Jail drinking what looked like a Magna Mocharetto with a bevy of guys. And once we crossed paths as he left the public library, trailing a cloud of air-conditioned calm. I was on my way in; he held the door for me.

The man I might someday come to admire would, I hoped, share this stranger's poise, his grace, and his deep vertical dimple.

With such secret thoughts, I shouldn't be surprised to hear my friend talk of Heroes. Yet if Ashleigh cherished a similar dream, I feared for her peace of mind. For is True Love likely to come to a high school sophomore who dresses in a chorus robe and ballet slippers?

"Okay, but listen, Ash," I said. "You're not planning to go to school wearing that, are you? No guy will even *look* at you." Me neither if they see me with you, I added inwardly. "Couldn't you please, please, please wear jeans?"

As always, my plea fell on deaf ears. "I see not the necessity of discussing with *you*, Miss Lefkowitz, the propriety of a young lady wearing Trousers. As you know, modesty forbids us to reveal the shape of the Lower Limbs."

If you do get a boyfriend, he's going to want to see a lot more than just the shape of your Lower Limbs, I argued silently. Fortunately, I reflected, the school year wouldn't start for another week—enough time, I hoped, to make her see reason.

"And don't you think you could call me Julie?" I continued. "We've known each other long enough, surely."

"My dearest Julia, you are right, indeed you are right. After all, in *Pride and Prejudice* Miss Elizabeth Bennet addresses her bosom friend, Miss Lucas, by the name of Charlotte, and they are no more affectionately attached than the two of us. But please, my dear friend, allow me to continue. As I said, I believe I have the solution to our puzzle of where to find our heroes."

"*Our* puzzle? It's not *my* puzzle," I put in.

Ashleigh shook me by the arm, letting her language slip a bit in her impatience. "Will you listen already? In *Pride and Prejudice*, where do the younger Bennet girls turn for lively masculine company? Why, to the regiment of soldiers quartered near their home. Were we to follow their lead, where better to seek suitors than among our neighboring young men in uniform?"

Could she be referring to the West Point cadets? The U.S. Military Academy at West Point sits high on a cliff overlooking the Hudson, hidden from Byzantium by the curve of the river. There brave and disciplined students train to lead our country's great army. Last year the center of the Byzantium Bullfrogs turned down Harvard to become a West Point cadet.

"Oh, Ashleigh, you've got to be kidding! You want us to go chasing after West Pointers? They're way too old! They've got crew cuts! You'll get us court-martialed!"

My friend held up her hand. "Hear me out, Julia," she said. "Hear me out. As you so rightly observe, the officers in training are not perfectly suited to ladies of our tender years. I propose instead another population of gentlemen in uniform—gentlemen younger than the cadets—I speak, in short, of the students at the Forefield Academy."

This suggestion was better, but only slightly. Forefield, an exclusive boys' prep school, rises above the town of Byzantium both geographically and socially. Its main building, once the mansion of the Forefield family, can be seen from most of the town, including my attic window. As a little girl I thought it was an enchanted castle, the home of a witch or a princess. I now considered it the home of gawky boys with crests embroidered on their blazer pockets—that is, of snobs, dorks, adders, or (most likely) snobbish, dorky adders.

"Forefield, huh? What's your plan? Are we going to dress up as boys and sneak in? Watch out—they'll see our lower limbs."

Flashing me a look of reproach and triumph, Ashleigh reached into her robe pocket and produced a piece of paper, which she silently handed to me. It appeared to be a page Xeroxed from a newspaper.

" 'Library Renovations,' " I read. " 'An extensive overhaul of Forefield's Robert Rive Science Library and Media Resource Center is on schedule for completion in time for the—' "

"No, not that. Underneath."

"What, this announcement? 'Forefield Fall Formal. The president and faculty of the Forefield Academy look forward to welcoming students, alumni, and their guests to the 97th annual Columbus Cotillion, at 8:00 P.M., Saturday, October 12. Formal attire.' Well, what good is that? We're not Forefield students, we're not alumni, and we're not their guests. We're not invited."

"Oh, that won't matter." Catching herself slipping into ordinary speech, Ashleigh began again. "I mean, That will be of no importance. With the crush of guests, two more will surely pass unnoticed."

"You want to crash the Snoot School Dork Dance? Are you out of your candy wrapper? What could that possibly have to do with Jane Austen?"

"Surely, Miss Lefkowitz, you can see that a gathering of young gentlemen dressed in formal attire, well practiced in time-honored dance steps, and unaccustomed to the company of young ladies—and therefore bound to treat us with modesty and respect—is the ideal place to meet our matches. Can you be blind to the perfection of the plan?"

Perfection! If the plan had any, I certainly was blind to it. In my experience, at least, boys who hadn't spent a lot of time around girls were less likely, not more, to behave themselves.

The sound of a maternal voice came faintly up the stairs.

"Is that Mrs. Lefkowitz calling?" said Ashleigh.

"Look—whatever you call me, you're *not* calling my mother Mrs. Lefkowitz. She didn't like it even when she was married to my father. If Helen isn't formal enough for you, call her Ms. Gould."

"I shall call her Madam."

Before I could make any further objections, the person in question knocked on the door.

"Come in," I called.

"Honey, I—oh, hi there, Ashleigh, you're here too. I was wondering. I thought I heard bouncing, but I didn't see you come in."

It astonishes Ashleigh and me that our parents have failed for so many years to notice how we use our tree.

"Good afternoon, Madam," answered Ashleigh.

"Excuseth me, Sir Ashleigh. I bid thee, too, the fairest of afternoons. Evenings, actually. Killed any dragons today?"

Ashleigh appeared too pained to reply. I took up her cause. "Mom, you're years out of date."

"Oho, years out of date, ameth I?" she said agreeably. "How canst thou tell—the grammar? I pray thee, forgive thine old, antiquated mommeth. Keeping up with the latest in teendom beeth too difficult for me. Dinnertime, honey. Ashleigh, you're welcome to join us."

"I thank you, Madam, but I knew not how far the day had advanced. My parents await me. Farewell." Curtsying to my mother, the Enthusiast tripped lightly down the stairs and took her leave.

Chapter 2

I seek Counsel ∽ a Domestic scene ∽ Dancing Lessons.

The next day was Tuesday, known in the Lefkowitz and Gould households as the Day of the Dad. I was glad. Not from any eagerness to spend time with my father, of course; relations between us have been strained ever since he left my mother and me for the Irresistible Accountant (or "Amy," as he prefers me to call her). Rather, I needed the advice of his next-door neighbor, the savviest person I know: Samantha Liu.

A visit to Dad and "Amy" often includes Samantha. Our fathers, both pediatricians, share a practice and a backyard hedge; Samantha's mother, an allergist, also shares the hedge, of course, but she has a separate medical practice. The long bicycle ride over gave me plenty of time to consider Ashleigh's wild plan. Though my father and stepmother didn't expect me until dinnertime, I started early, hoping to find Samantha free for a chat. Some subjects are best discussed in person—particularly those subjects that live a mere tree's breadth away from me. From time to time, Ashleigh and I overhear each other's phone conversations.

I was in luck: Samantha was home. Once we had installed ourselves comfortably in the Lius' hammock with a pair of ginger ales, I opened my heart.

"Okay, Sam, warm up the advice generator," I entreated.

"What's up? Stepmother trouble again?"

"No—at least, not yet. I haven't seen 'Amy' for a week. Right now it's Ashleigh."

At that name, Samantha gave an affectionate, twinkly grimace. It always surprises me that the two of them like each other as much as they do. Samantha is more than a year older and at least a millennium more mature. Ashleigh's reputation for eccentricity prevents her from rising to the upper circles of our high school world, even if she wanted to. Samantha, on the other hand, enjoys the status of a gymnast, a beauty, last year's president of the sophomore class, and the sister of the famously hot Zach Liu, still an object of near-universal fantasy even though he graduated last year. In fact, it's a measure of Samantha's social standing that she can afford to be gracious to someone as odd as Ashleigh (or, I often think, me). Yet Sam is loyal and, though skilled at manipulation, essentially kind.

"What is it this time?" she asked. "Let me guess: Ashleigh's taken over your bathtub for her starfish collection? She's excavating an emerald mine under your basement and you're afraid your house will collapse? No, wait, I know—she's decided to go to school every day dressed as Martha Washington."

With such intuition, is it any wonder Sam is so successful?

"You got the first problem right on the nose," I said. "Well, the left nostril. Not Martha Washington, Jane Austen—close enough, though. Jane Austen doesn't involve a white wig, which makes her a bit better, I guess. Ash is refusing to wear anything but a long skirt. No jeans, no pants—she doesn't want her 'lower limbs' to show."

"Oh, dear. I take it you've tried reasoning with her? Told her no one will sit next to her in homeroom and so on?"

"When did Ashleigh ever listen to reason? Besides, she knows *I'll* sit next to her."

"Well, you might not be in her homeroom this year, but I see your point. And begging didn't work either, right?"

"Of course not."

"Could you move her on to a new fad—get her interested in rooting for the football team or something?"

I paused to smile at the thought of Ashleigh rooting for the football team. "This *is* a new fad, unfortunately. It started yesterday. It replaces the Wet Blankets."

"Then you'll just have to bargain with her. Refuse to do something she wants unless she agrees to wear normal clothes. In the meantime, maybe you can find some sort of in-between outfit that would work for either era. A long black skirt or an Indian print, something like that. That way, even though she might not look crisp, at least she won't look insane. Tell you what, if you don't find an effective threat by the weekend, let me know and I'll get a few of the girls on the gymnastics team to come to school in long skirts on Monday, so Ashleigh won't be the only one."

A generous offer! No one, however fond of gossip, could blame a sophomore for dressing like the gymnasts, the most successful athletes at Byz High. Last year the girls' gymnastics team placed first in twice as many meets as the football and basketball teams combined won games. They were the pride of the school and the leaders of fashion.

"But I didn't tell you the worst part yet," I continued. "Ashleigh's planning to crash a dance at the Forefield Academy, and she wants me to come with her."

Samantha gave a thumbs-up with her ginger-ale can. "There you go! Tell her you'll go only if she gives up the weird wardrobe."

"No way, Sam! You want me to crash a dance at Snoot School? I'll die of embarrassment."

"Face it, Julie, you know you're going to end up going anyway. You can never say no to Ashleigh. You might as well get something out of it this time."

Much as I hated to admit it, she had a point. I finished my ginger ale, thanked her, and made my way to my father's house.

⌒∘

After we finished our dinner of grilled chicken breast marinated in pomegranate juice and spinach-walnut salad with orange vinaigrette—my stepmother is a skillful if fussy cook—Ashleigh called. She was buzzing with news of some sort.

I told her I would discuss it tomorrow and hung up hastily. The Irresistible Accountant disapproves of teenagers talking on the telephone. She especially disapproves of Ashleigh. Having extracted my father from his messy life, she wants to simplify and straighten out the only aspect that he couldn't entirely leave behind: me. In her view, Ashleigh belongs to the world of mess. Amy much prefers Samantha, holding her up as an example of ideal girlhood. Although the feeling isn't mutual, Samantha always advises me to keep the peace with my stepmother. Ash, in contrast, speaks her mind and encourages me to speak mine.

"Was that Ashleigh on the phone, sweetie?" asked Amy. "I wish you would ask that girl not to call during family time. Your father and I only get to see you for a few precious hours a week. I think it's very inconsiderate of her not to respect that."

Yeah, you wouldn't want to waste a precious minute that you could be spending picking at me and criticizing my friends. This

is what I did *not* say to Amy. If I had a dollar for every sharp remark I keep to myself, I would be able to fund the Stepfamily
Peace Prize, my dream version of the Nobel, to be awarded an-
nually to the person who displays the greatest familial restraint.
I considered it especially unfair that, having voluntarily given up
the pleasure of talking to Ashleigh, I should still have to listen to
my stepmother's complaints, just as if Ash and I had yapped
away on the phone for hours.

"Don't you agree, Steve?" said my stepmother.

"Hmm? Yes, of course," said my father, getting up and heading to his study. He stopped on the way to kiss his wife on the top
of her head. "I love to see my two favorite girls together. You two
sit here, relax, and catch up."

I waited until the door had swung shut behind him, then took
my bag and headed upstairs to "my" room, which I share with
the I.A.'s sewing machine. The knowledge that she has an excuse
to enter at any moment makes the room feel less than comfortable and far from private. Still, at least I would be alone there.

"Where are you going, sweetie?" she asked.

"Homework."

"How can you have homework when school doesn't start for
another week?"

"Summer reading," I lied. (I had already finished the assigned
book—*Lord of the Flies*—back in June.)

"Really? What are they having you read? Let's see," she said,
reaching for my book. "Oh, you lucky girl—Jane Austen, *Sense
and Sensibility*! I loved that book. She's my favorite writer. The
romance between your father and me was straight out of an
Austen novel."

Right, like Jane Austen wrote about igsome schemers who

steal other people's husbands, I didn't say. I awarded myself an imaginary dollar for refraining, bringing the total for the evening up to two dollars, and escaped upstairs.

∽

When I got home the next morning, I slipped next door in search of news. Finding Ashleigh still asleep, I pounced on her toes.

She gave a most satisfactory squeal. "Juniper, get *off*!" she cried, mistaking me for her kitten.

Mewing and pinching, I attempted to keep her in the dark as to my true identity. Pretty soon, however, she stopped thrashing blindly, opened her eyes, and identified me as a member of the Human Race.

"Oh, it's you. What are you doing up so early? What time is it?"

"Long past a bat's bedtime. Get up, lazybones!"

Ashleigh buried her head under her pillow.

I like morning. It's the only time when *my* enthusiasm outstrips *hers*.

"Fine, I guess you don't want to tell me your news then," I said, making a feint toward the window. That roused her. She sprang out of bed—or, more accurately, she rose with a speed somewhat greater than that of a daffodil emerging from the moist earth in March. In a mere twenty minutes she had put on a selection of interesting clothes and her Austenesque manner.

"Let us repair to your abode, where there is more room, my dear Miss Lefkowitz—"

"You mean your dear Julie—"

"Quite right, my dearest Julia—Let us repair to your abode, where there is more room."

"More room for what?" I asked, retreating through the window. Ashleigh followed me out. Our rooms are more or less the same size, but in the course of her enthusiasms Ashleigh has accumulated far more stuff than I have. In particular, one large papier-mâché dragon hanging from the ceiling tends to bump you on the head if you try to walk across her room without looking both ways first. Well, it bumps *me*, anyway.

"Dancing lessons, Twinkle-Toes," she explained, diving through my window and landing on my bed. "If we are to discharge our duties as party guests with the dignity that befits our position as Ladies, we must learn to perform the required steps. I have here a book"—she thumped the pillow with it—"that promises to instruct us in the Art of Terpsichore."

"Whoa there! You want us to learn how to dance by reading a book called *The Art of Sick Twerpery*? Have you lost your lemon drops?"

"Not sick twerpery—Terpsichore. Terpsichore, the Muse of Dance. It is she who breathes life into the Limbs of the Dancers as they perform their graceful movements." She flung her arms out to demonstrate; a series of crashes followed. Luckily, nothing broke.

"Very graceful," I said, putting my desk lamp back on my desk. "Okay, so you want us to learn to dance by reading a book called *The Art of Terpsichore*?"

"No, no, 'the Art of Terpsichore' is merely a description of the book's contents. The volume itself is called *Dancing*. To be precise, *Dancing and Its Relations to Education and Social Life, with a New Method of Instruction, Including a Complete Guide to the Cotillion (German) with 250 Figures*. By Allen Dodworth. Published in New York, 1888. New and Enlarged Edition."

"I don't care what it's called, you can't learn to dance by reading a book."

"Yes, you can. It has 250 figures. See?" She opened the book to show me.

" 'Number Forty-eight. The Inconstants,' " I read. " 'Three couples.—They arrange themselves in a phalanx behind the conducting couple; the first gentleman turns round, giving his left arm, crossed at the elbow, to the left arm of the gentleman behind him, with whom he changes places and partners; he goes on without interruption to the last lady; when he reaches the last, the second gentleman, who is then at the head of the phalanx, executes the same figure, and so on for the rest, until every one has regained his place; general waltz follows.' Well, that's as clear as crumb cake."

"Nonsense, it's perfectly simple. The first gentleman goes like this, then the second gentleman goes like that, then he takes the lady's arm, and they go like this, and meanwhile the third gentleman goes like that, and the lady goes like this, and the other couple does the same thing, and then they all dance. Come on, try it, it'll be fun."

I picked up my desk lamp and put it back on my desk again. "That's a dance for three couples," I said. "Maybe we should start with something for one couple." I paged through the book. " 'The Galop, the Racket, the Esmeralda (or Three-Slide Polka), the Minuet, the Lancers, the Quadrille.' You realize, don't you, that nobody dances these things nowadays? We'd be better off learning the fox trot or the twist. Or just figuring out how to wiggle with dignity."

"Fox Trot? Faugh! Elizabeth Bennet and Fitzwilliam Darcy never danced any such thing. That's a Twentieth-Century dance."

"Well, what makes you think they danced the Esmeralda? This book was published in 1888—that's a good seventy-five years after *Pride and Prejudice*."

"Okay, perhaps not the Esmeralda," said Ashleigh, "but they're always talking about the Lancers. Let's learn that."

"Right, the Lancers. Ever popular with the crisp crowd. Kids were trampling each other to get to the dance floor when they started to play it at last year's prom."

Ash shot me her Scornful Look. Taking Mr. Dodworth's volume in one hand, she began reading minuet instructions aloud while prancing up and down the room. For a third time I returned my lamp to its place on the desk. It was a bit dented, but the lightbulb was intact.

My mother put her head in the door. "I take it Ashleigh's here?" she said. "Hello, Ashleigh. Funny, I never hear you come in. Broken anything?"

"Nothing important," I assured her.

"Ah, Ms. Gould! Just whom I most wished to see! Do us the kindness to step over here, Madam," cried Ashleigh, taking my mother by the elbow. "We are short a couple. Would you rather be a Gentleman dancing with an imaginary Lady, or a Lady with an imaginary Gentleman?"

"The lady with the imaginary gentleman, I think—that's pretty much how things stand anyway, so it won't take much imagination," said Mom. "What are we dancing?"

"The minuet," answered Ashleigh, showing Mom the book.

"Don't you think it would be easier with music?" suggested my mother. She turned to me. "Run and get the Mozart string quartets from the dining room, honey—oh, and grab some Strauss too, in case we want to waltz. Ashleigh, want to give me a hand with the desk? If we push it under the eaves, you might stop running into it."

My mother was right to take charge. She turned out to be an excellent dancer. Who would have guessed? Ducking from time to time when a turn took us too close to the slanting roof, we mastered the three essential movements—the walk, the slide, and the balancé. Then we practiced combining them into various figures of the quadrille. Another surprise: this turns out to be nothing but a slightly-less-dorky square dance. We made a stab at the minuet, which is a bit more complicated, and rounded off the lesson with a waltz.

"There," said Ashleigh, after my mother had left. "Now we will indeed be ready for the Forefield ball, where I, like Elizabeth Bennet, will find my heart's mate—my Mr. Darcy. And you, like Jane Bennet, will find your Mr. Bingley."

I bristled inwardly. I could understand how Ashleigh might identify with Elizabeth Bennet, that lively-minded young lady, though to me she seems more like one of Elizabeth's flighty younger sisters. But I was a little offended at her equating me with dull, good Jane, who falls in love with the second-rate Mr. Bingley. Though well meaning and well off, Bingley doesn't have half the brains or one-tenth the inner strength (not to mention the income) of proud, handsome Mr. Darcy, Elizabeth's suitor. It seemed doubly unfair that Ashleigh should intend to hog Mr. Darcy when I was the one who gave her the book in the first place. But I suppressed my annoyance and opened negotiations to crash the dance with Ash, in return for her promise to dress like a normal human being during school hours.

Chapter 3

Ball Gowns ∾ Footwear ∾ Barns ∾ A Masked Man.

*O*ur next task was to find suitable clothing for the dance. Fortunately, help was close at hand: my mother's shop, where she
sells dainty objects such as greeting cards, teacups, beeswax can-
dles, and—most important—vintage clothes.

Before my father left, Helen's Treasures occupied our front
parlor and served as a hobby for my mother, offering its antique
footstools and potpourri to weekend visitors with noses of steel.
Now the shop's tentacles reach back through the entire ground
floor. Even in the kitchen, I have to push aside boxes of scented
soap whenever I need an onion.

Despite the expansion, however, Helen's Treasures is not a fi-
nancial success. A painter, art teacher, and waitress before she
married my father, Mom has more artistic talent than business
smarts. Helen's Treasures makes just barely enough for our
expenses—that is, if you factor in alimony too.

Ashleigh and I spent the last two weekdays before school
started helping out in the shop: sorting, taking inventory, and re-
placing the unsold summer merchandise with fall items. In return, Mom offered us our choice of the vintage clothing.

Ashleigh rummaged through the dresses and pulled out a

pair of matching fluffy pink things that some long-ago bride had inflicted on her bridesmaids. "Aren't these perfect?" she cried.

I was incensed. "Are you missing your macaroons? Crashing the dance is bad enough. I draw the line at crashing in a clown suit."

"Although perhaps a little more pink than is strictly desirable, these dresses are modest and seemly," countered Ash. "Do you have a better idea?"

"How about a couple of blouses and our long black skirts from chorus?"

"Unthinkable! Insufficiently formal for a formal!"

As we argued, I remembered that we still had a trunk to unpack from one of Mom's estate liquidations. We opened it and hit pay dirt—dresses from long ago in many hues and sizes.

I chose a sleeveless gown of silver-gray satin that matched my eyes and brought out the golden highlights in my hair. It fell in pools and folds like the drapery of a classical statue; for once I looked graceful instead of bony. A line of glittering rhinestones accentuated my collarbones. The gray went well with the black onyx of my lucky thumb ring, I thought.

Ashleigh picked a frock of deep crimson silk, the rustly kind, whose tight waist, low V-neck, and full skirt showed off her figure. The red suited her curly black hair and dark eyes. We each added a wrap—mine satin to match my dress, hers cashmere trimmed in black mink, shedding a little.

One problem still remained: what to wear on our feet. I had grown so much over the summer that even my sneakers had started to pinch. My old dress flats, scuffed and childish, were fortunately far too small. As for Ashleigh, a tomboy till last Monday, she had never owned any feminine footwear. Although we found a number of vintage shoes among my mother's things, none of them fit us.

Clearly we both needed new shoes. "Let's get your mom to take us to the mall on Saturday," I suggested. "Mine can't leave Treasures on the weekend—that's when she makes most of her sales."

To my surprise, Ashleigh objected. "We will be wearing long dresses, as befits ladies," she said. "Nobody will see our shoes."

"They will if we're dancing," I pointed out.

"Not if we dance with dignity," she answered.

Dignity? Ashleigh? A laughable concept. Ashleigh's attitude puzzled me. Shopping may not be our favorite activity in the world, but we like it fine, and it certainly seemed necessary now. After some probing, however, I discovered what held her back: empathy. Ashleigh's easygoing, indulgent, and well-to-do parents kept their only child supplied with everything she needed, and a great many things she merely wanted. For me, it was more complicated. My mother would give me what I needed if I asked for it, but I hated to ask, knowing how our budget would suffer. My father, on the other hand, had plenty of money, but I couldn't stand to ask him for it. Not only was I too proud, but I wanted to protect my mother from looking incapable. As for the money I'd earned over the summer scooping ice cream at Conehead's, I'd earmarked that for more urgent wardrobe needs.

Out of loyalty, Ashleigh hesitated to buy new shoes when I couldn't. I was touched, but I urged her to reconsider. Ashleigh being Ashleigh, she wouldn't budge.

"The problem is clearly beyond us," she said. "We must consult a Higher Authority. Call Sam."

"I know you're not going to like this," Sam told me when I

reached her on her cell phone, "but the answer is Amy. She has plenty of money and perfect taste. Don't waste perfectly good parental guilt. If my father left my mother for a younger woman, I'd have a pair of Manolos for each toe. Get Amy to take you shopping for shoes, and tell her it was Ashleigh's idea to ask her for help. She'll be flattered—maybe she'll like Ashleigh better. Two good results for the price of one. I'm going to the mall myself tomorrow, to shop for uniforms with the gymnastics team. If you go then, you can give me a ride home afterward."

∽

I asked Amy to pick us up behind Ashleigh's house on Saturday morning, not wanting my mother to see my father's SUV. I hadn't mentioned my stepmother's involvement to Mom, explaining simply that I was going shopping with Ashleigh.

My stepmother and my friend were on their best behavior. Amy called us both sweetie and warned Ashleigh only twice to keep her feet off the seats. Ash, for her part, took pains to support my claim that she admired Amy's taste, by complimenting her on her haircut, her handbag, her shoes, and her sunglasses. She stopped only after I kicked her hard.

Conversation was strained at first. Topic after topic fizzled after a sentence or two. Things perked up a bit when Ashleigh hit on bird watching, pointing out what she claimed were red-tailed hawks, a pair of falcons, and a bald eagle—which I maintained were crows, ducks, and a seagull.

"A seagull? Faugh! What would a seagull be doing so far from the sea?"

"They come up the Hudson. You've seen them a million times."

"We have left the Hudson far behind us. Do you think me unable to recognize the National Bird of Our Great Nation? Look, there it is again!"

Amy refused to be drawn into the dispute. "I couldn't say, girls," she said when we appealed to her. "I didn't see it. I have to keep my eyes on the road."

We were all relieved to arrive at the mall, where we began our search at the Teen Barn. (All right, it's not really called that, but why should I provide them with free publicity after the way the last three things I bought there fell apart in the wash? And why, by the way, must every shop bill itself as a Barn, a Warehouse, a Depot, or a Garage? Who'd want to buy their clothes in a garage?)

Shopping with Amy was nothing like shopping with Ashleigh or my mother. *We* prefer to linger and laugh, leaving at last with at least one ill-judged purchase to be returned later, when we come to our senses. Still, much as it chilled me, I admired Amy's efficiency. The Irresistible One plucked shoes from the racks as a magician does rabbits. From her suggestions, I chose a pair of silver-gray pumps that I knew would go beautifully with my silver gown. Ashleigh wanted a red pair, but agreed to black.

Amy also bought me several pairs of new pants, pointing out with disapproval that my legs had grown several inches, as if it was something I could help. She seemed to know what would fit and flatter without so much as a glance at the tags. Her narrow heels clicked on the linoleum like fingernails on a keyboard. In record time she had me outfitted for the winter.

"Okay, girls, I have a manicure appointment," she said when we were done. "Come and get me in an hour. Remember we promised to give Samantha a ride home too. Call my cell phone if you need me. Is your phone on, sweetie? Have fun," she said, kissing me on the forehead. I suppressed a flinch and waved good-bye as the Demon of Efficiency clicked her way out of sight behind the fountain.

Ashleigh and I spent the next hour wandering happily from Barn to Barn. In the Candy Barn we played Sherlock Nose, a game Ashleigh invented years ago, in which one player blindfolds the other and takes her on a tour of jellybean bins until the blindfolded one has correctly identified seven flavors in a row.

After they kicked us out, we visited the Game Barn, where Ashleigh pestered the staff with requests for the official rules to Loo, Vingt-et-un, Casino, Lottery Tickets, Picquet, Whist, and Fish, which the alert Jane Austen reader will recognize as the names of card games played by characters in Miss Austen's novels.

The Game Barn staff, evidently, were not Jane Austen readers.

After they kicked us out, we retreated to the Book Barn, where, for a change, they let us browse our fill. Ashleigh bought her own copy of *Pride and Prejudice*, as well as *Love and Freindship*, Jane Austen's very first novel, written when she was just our age and not very good at spelling.

Then Ash wanted to play video games. Fearing for my nerves, I went to see if Sam had arrived yet at our rendezvous point, the Sports Barn.

I found her just as she left her fellow gymnasts. I saw their supple backs as they strode away.

"Oh, hey," she greeted me. "Where's Ashleigh and Amy?"

"Ash is in the Arcade Barn shooting alien starships, or enemy soldiers, or fish in a barrel, or something. She'll be here when she runs out of quarters," I replied. "The I.A. is having her talons painted red. I think she wanted to get away from Ashleigh."

"Oh, dear. Friction?"

"Not so bad, really. They kept it polite."

"I can just imagine."

"On the bright side, if Ash hadn't come along, I'd probably still be stuck with the I.A., having some sort of horrible just-us-girls version of Family Time. What is it with that?"

Sam made a sympathetic face. "Right, the maternal thing. You know why she does that, don't you?"

"Not really," I said. "She's not stupid—can't she tell I don't like her? And it's not like *she* likes *me*, either. Does she think it'll please my father, or is she just trying to torture me?"

"Maybe a little. But mostly I think her deal is, she really wants children and she's afraid she can't have any. She thinks you're all she'll get."

"Ig," I said. I couldn't decide which was worse, being stuck as Amy's substitute daughter or having a little half-sibling, with Amy contributing the other half.

Sam changed the subject: "Hey, speaking of ig, want to see something funny?" She steered me past aisles of fleece and spandex. "They've got sample team uniforms in here that must go back to at least the 1920s. There—just look at that!" She held out a little pleated dress with puff sleeves. Pinned to the bottom of the skirt was a pair of bloomers. "What kind of sado-coach would make a team wear *that*?"

We spent some moments urging each other to try on the worst of the samples. When a saleslady headed our way, however, with "Can I help you?" on her lips and murder in her eye, we made for the calmer waters of the Aquatics Department.

But before we could reach the kayaks, we found our way blocked by a figure in a close-fitting white jacket, smooth across the chest. Matching trousers fit snugly as well, showing off his powerful thighs. His face was hidden under what looked like a wire colander. In his hand he held a sword, which he was using to menace a large inflatable frog.

Samantha cleared her throat.

The warrior sprang to attention. With one graceful movement he brought his sword down and touched the blade to his forehead. Then, sweeping off his mask, he stood aside and bowed silently.

As he rose from his courtesy, I found myself staring transfixed, eyes locked with the blazing turquoise eyes of my Mysterious Stranger.

For a moment I stood and stared. Then Sam said, "Oh, hi," breaking the spell. The Stranger smiled at her, showing the tips of his beautiful white teeth. He bowed again slightly and withdrew.

Feeling weak and trembly, I breathed, "Samantha, who was that Masked Man?"

"Some guy from Zach's dojo," she answered. "I don't remember his name. I think they might have had kendo together."

"Kendo?"

"Japanese sword fighting. I was considering trying it myself, but Zach thinks I'd like aikido better."

Shyness prevented me from asking Samantha any more questions about the Stranger. She continued to weigh the relative merits of the various martial arts, but I can't tell you what she said. Indeed, the rest of the afternoon passed as in a dream, those turquoise eyes always before my inner eyes. All the way home Ashleigh called seagulls eagles to her heart's content while Sam entertained my stepmother with details of team uniforms, without any interference from me.

Chapter 4

Tenth Grade ↜ Extracurriculars ↜ A Sonnet.

*T*he dream faded soon enough, however, and I awoke to the cold, hard knowledge that summer was over. I speak metaphorically, of course. Actually it was still pretty hot out, especially in my attic bedroom. Mom is always promising to redo the insulation if business ever picks up.

Monday morning Mom made me my traditional back-to-school breakfast: whole-wheat buttermilk waffles with maple syrup and homemade sour cherry jam. (Ashleigh's candy-making phase had a strong jam component.) For an extra treat, Mom set the table downstairs in the front parlor, at a claw-footed oak table that's been on sale for several years. If it ever does sell, I'll miss it terribly.

I brushed my hair quickly, put on my lucky thumb ring, and came downstairs. I was wearing some of the clothes my stepmother had provided, and I worried a little that my mother would notice and ask where they had come from. Indeed, she looked me up and down appraisingly. All she said, though, was, "How nice you look, honey."

At school, Ash and I were disappointed to find we had different homerooms. She drew Frau Riechstoff-Murphy, the

German teacher, and I landed the notorious math teacher Mr. Klamp.

Mr. Klamp laid down the law. No tardiness, no talking above 40 decibels, no untied shoelaces, no visible undergarments, no eating, no chewing gum, no chewing tobacco, no chewing betel nuts, no chewing coca leaves, no chewing out students (unless Mr. Klamp was doing the chewing out), no chewing out teachers (unless ditto), no unnecessary displays of temper (unless ditto), no unnecessary displays of affection (no exceptions), no pets over one ounce or under one ton, and no singing, except in Bulgarian. I began to think Mr. Klamp wouldn't be so bad—which was lucky, since I had him for math as well.

This year, the social highlights of my homeroom included three of the grade's five Seths; Tall Alex and Mad Alex; Michelle Jeffries; Cordelia Nixon; and one of the Gerard twins—Yolanda or Yvette.

The Y girls are identical twins: the same light-footed roundness, tapered fingers, smooth, dark skin, and elegantly swooping nostrils. Like many identical twins, they like to confuse people by playing games with their clothes and hairstyles. One favorite trick involves gradually trading the colored beads at the ends of their braids, so that, for example, Yolanda will start off with nothing but yellow and Yvette with nothing but green. By the end of the week they'll both be fifty-fifty yellow and green. Then comes the tricky part. One twin will gradually acquire all the yellow beads and the other all the green—but is the green twin Yolanda, taking over her sister's look, or is it Yvette, returning to her original color?

Fortunately—or unfortunately, I guess, if you're a Gerard twin—there's a simple way for those in the know to tell whether someone is Yolanda or Yvette. Just stand near her and wait. If the twin in question starts to talk, there's a good chance it's Yolanda. If she goes on talking for three or four sentences, the good chance becomes a certainty. Yolanda once told me in confidence that in her elementary school, they used to call her Yoyo Mouth.

"Julie Lefkowitz! Look at you! You got so tall! Are you taking physics this year? Let's see your schedule. Look, we're in gym together. And English—Ms. Nettleton, ig. No fair! I heard we were supposed to get Ms. Muchnick, everybody says she's loudly crisp, but she had to go get pregnant. Why would she want a baby when she could have had *us*? Hey, did you do the summer reading? They love *Lord of the Flies*, don't they? We had it in eighth grade at Sacred Heart, and the next summer in Enrichment. If I have to read it one more time, I'm going to go throw myself off a cliff. They call that book realistic? If you ask me, not even boys would act that way. Speaking of boys, here comes Seth Young! Hey, Seth Young! Where've you been all summer? Let's see your schedule. Did you hear about Muchnick?" Diagnosis: Yolanda.

For the first few days, school had an air of embarrassed festivity. Everyone had come back from their vacations taller, stronger, gawkier, slimmed down or curvier, with their hair grown past their shoulders or newly cropped and sticking out funny. The lawyers' sons had deep tans from their wilderness adventures, the hippie farmers' daughters from their long days working outdoors. The cliques shimmered like a mirage, and for a moment it seemed as if a former nerd might cross unharmed into the crisp crowd. Then the walls firmed up again and the moment passed.

"Julie, it's time for you to start thinking seriously about college," said my father one Tuesday evening. "Your grades are good, but that's not enough. Admissions officers are going to want to see strong extracurriculars too. I know you like to write. Have you thought about joining the school newspaper? Or what about the literary magazine?"

I groaned silently. The editors of the *Byzantine Bugle* publish enthusiastic little stories about pep rallies and food drives. Everything has to pass the scrutiny of the administration; the result is loudly dull. The literary magazine, *Sailing to Byzantium*, isn't so bad—at least, it wasn't so bad last year, when Ms. Muchnick was the adviser. With the Much on maternity leave, though, Ms. Nettleton had taken over. Three periods a week of *her* was quite enough for *me*.

"I don't know, Dad," I said. "I'm pretty busy with school, plus there's my job at Conehead's." (I decided not to tell him that, due to a weather-linked decrease in the demand for frozen treats, Conehead's had let me go for the winter.) "Anyway, I'm just not into the whole newspaper/magazine thing so much."

"You know I wish you'd give up that job," said Dad. "Conehead's isn't exactly the most impressive credential to have on your record. What about student government or science club? That might be even better than the newspaper. The admissions officers like to see well-rounded students."

Well rounded! I glanced ruefully at my bony knees. Which, I wondered, would be worse: to tell my father that a midlevel nobody like me had no chance whatsoever of winning a school government election—essentially a popularity contest—or to express distaste for science, his favorite subject and the basis of his career? For the thousandth time, I envied girls whose fathers had a clue about their interests and personalities. Banking two imaginary dollars in the Familial Restraint Fund, I told Dad I would think about it.

And I did. What I thought was this: If there were justice in the world, the hours I spent with Ashleigh would count as an extracurricular activity. Science Club, History Club, and Future Candy Makers of America, all smushed together and laid out to dry like a Fruit Roll-Up.

❧

Autumn blew in cold and clear the next week. As the days grew shorter and their hours grew longer, we settled down in earnest to tenth grade.

In Mrs. Marlin's class, Charlemagne advanced across Europe (or do I mean retreated?), followed (or perhaps preceded) by his ancestors, descendants, henchmen, or enemies, Clovis, Childeric, and Pepin the Short. (History was never my thing. Unlike English, where you can make things up, or math, where you can figure things out, history depends on happening to know what happens to have happened. Where's the sense in *that*?)

In English, the only class I had with Ashleigh, the vicious children of Summer Reading—I refer to the characters in *Lord of the Flies*, not my classmates—made way for Shakespeare's unfortunate lovers.

"How do we know that Romeo and Juliet are in love?" asked Ms. Nettleton one rainy third period. "Yes, Julie?"

"Shakespeare tells us in the prologue. He calls them 'A pair of star-cross'd lovers' and talks about 'The fearful passage of their death-mark'd love,' " I said.

You'd think any teacher would be thrilled to have evidence that a student had read and understood the homework. Not Ms.

Nettleton. When she asks a question, she doesn't want just any answer; she's interested only in the one *she'd* give.

"Yes, but what clues does Shakespeare give in the dialogue itself? Anyone? Not you, Seth, I know you know. Peter?"

"When Juliet goes, 'Romeo, Romeo, oh, wherefore art thou, Romeo?' " said Peter the Short.

Ms. Nettleton squinted at him mistrustfully. That line doesn't appear until the next week's reading, and Peter is not the type to read ahead. She clearly suspected him of winging it. "Before that. At the dance—the Capulet party, where Romeo and Juliet meet. Did anyone notice anything special about the first words they say to each other?"

"They're kind of flirting," said Yolanda. "They're kissing each other's hands and things."

"Yes, but what about the *form* of the lines? Did anything look familiar from our unit last year on poetry? Anyone? All right, Seth, tell the class."

"They speak in rhyme and meter," said Seth Young. "In fact, the first part of their conversation takes the form of a sonnet."

"Thank you, Seth," said Ms. Nettleton. She wrote *sonnet* on the blackboard and started explaining in words as dull as they were informative. From rhyme schemes she proceeded to iambic pentameter, fourteen lines, final couplets. The bell rang before we got back to Romeo's feelings for Juliet, or vice versa.

"Who *cares* if it's a sonnet?" said Yolanda as we made our way to the cafeteria. "That whole love-at-first-sight thing is a pile of crock, anyway. Okay, it's better than *Lord of the Flies*, but not much. Romeo's already in love before he meets Juliet—with that Rosalind person, who's her *cousin*, mega-ig. Then he sees Juliet and he's all 'Let me kiss your hand, I really mean it this

time, you know I do 'cause I'm telling you in a *sonnet.*' And
Juliet's not even *fourteen* yet. He's going to kill himself over an
eighth grader? Yeah, right."

Ashleigh disagreed. While not every pair of lovers understood the true nature of their attachment at the moment of their
first meeting, she maintained, some did. She gave as an example
of the former type, Elizabeth Bennet and her Mr. Darcy; of the
latter type, Elizabeth's sister Jane and her Mr. Bingley. Finding
that Yolanda had not yet read *Pride and Prejudice,* she jumped at
the chance to describe it.

In the meantime I chewed my egg salad in silence, thinking
about the nature of love.

Two people could know each other for years, I reflected, and
promise to love each other forever, yet find their hearts and interests at odds. That was certainly the case with my parents.
However, the example of the Drs. Liu suggested that lasting love
did sometimes blossom from the first encounter. Samantha's parents met in a singing group—Haichang has a baritone voice, Lily
a sweet mezzo-soprano—and they still put their cheeks together
and croon in harmony whenever they think nobody's around.

What, I wondered, would be *my* fate in love?

If Ashleigh was right, I would find out soon enough. Only a
week remained until the Forefield Columbus Cotillion. We had
rehearsed our dance steps until we could confidently hop
through three flavors of quadrille, a minuet, and the Sir Roger de
Coverly, as well as the fox trot, the waltz, and some simple swing.
We had even practiced wiggling freestyle. I felt we were as ready
as we ever would be.

First, however, we had an obstacle to overcome: how to get there. Ash and I hesitated to ask our parents to drive us to the dance—we were afraid they might somehow figure out that we hadn't, in fact, been invited. In the end, we decided it would be best not to tell them about it at all. We would let them think we had gone to the movies with Sam. ("Wearing ballgowns?" objected Ashleigh. —"You've dragged me to the movies wearing far worse," I answered.) That left a choice of walking the three miles to Forefield or riding our bicycles up the long hill, catching our hems in the gears and arriving in a sweat. Our return seemed even more problematic.

Once again, Sam came to our aid—or, more precisely, her brother, Zach, home from college for the Columbus Day weekend. When I went to the Lius' house to borrow a pair of evening purses from Sam's large collection, she offered us Zach's services as a chauffeur. "I told him if he didn't drive you, you'd get tangled in your bike pedals and wind up in a ditch with a broken neck. Then your father would die of a broken heart and Dad would have to find a new partner. Zach said you were idiots, but he'd do it for the family honor. He likes an excuse to drive that car of his."

"Thanks—I guess. You sure you don't want to come?"

Samantha laughed. "Can you see me chasing boys at the Forehead Academy? The guys I already know are quite enough for me, thanks. Have a good time, and don't let Ashleigh do anything too embarrassing."

Chapter 5

A ride through the Dark ❧ A menacing adder ❧
A gallant rescue ❧ A Quadrille ❧ A Waltz ❧ A second Sonnet.

Zach picked us up at Ashleigh's house. "Ready for the costume party, kids?" he said.

"It's not a costume party, it's the Columbus Cotillion," said Ash, getting in the front. "And we're hardly kids."

Zach headed uphill along the river. "Hmm," he said, looking her over critically. "You're right, you don't look so kidlike in that dress. Those boys at the Foreplay Academy better watch out."

Ashleigh slapped at his shoulder. He grabbed her wrist with three fingers and started to twist. "Hey! Guys! Keep your eyes on the road," I said.

My stomach fluttered as we turned off the river road and drove up the twisting approach toward the Forefield gate. In my long friendship with Ashleigh, I had become accustomed to a certain level of public attention. When your best friend goes around town dressed in armor constructed from cookware, eyes naturally turn your way. But getting thrown out of the Candy Barn for sniffing too many jellybeans is one thing; marching boldly into a nest of reputed snobs while dressed in ancient frocks that smell faintly of mothballs kicks up the potential for embarrassment to a whole new level.

"Let us off here, Zach," I said. "We'll walk the rest of the way. It'll be easier to get in if we kind of edge along behind some other people." Zach got out to open the rear door, which sticks from the inside.

"Okay, kids—ladies. Call me when you've had enough. And tell me if any of those Foureyes kids get fresh—I'll kick their asses." He demonstrated with a carefully placed karate kick that fortunately left no mark on the back of my silver dress, then drove off into the night.

Ashleigh and I gathered up our skirts and edged through the gate to the Forefield Academy, our heels sinking into the grass by the side of the drive. The air was sharp; I pulled my wrap around my shoulders. Carved lions observed us from either side of the gate, their tails curled catlike around their flanks, their noses lifted in stony disdain, as if we weren't worth the effort of a pounce. Two or three cars whished slowly by, fluttering my hair and Ashleigh's sash.

We reached the top of the hill and began to pass the school buildings, each more imposing than the last. After a minute or two we drew near enough to hear fragments of music trickling across the lawns from the old Forefield mansion, the heart of the academy. As soon as I saw it, I recognized it as the palace visible from my attic. From close up it looked at once more real and more enchanted. Light spilled out through tall windows and laughter mingled with the music. It sounded elegant and merry, utterly unlike the noisy chaos that passed for dances in the Byz High gym.

Ashleigh was all for charging up the broad marble steps to the door, but I held her back. We waited until a group of partygoers came up behind us, then hurried through the door at their heels, hoping any observers would think we were with them.

No such luck. At the entrance a red-faced man, gaunt yet jowly, sat behind a table taking tickets. "Excuse me! Excuse me, girls! Tickets?" he honked at us as we tried to sneak past.

Ashleigh opened the black beaded evening bag Sam had lent her, peered in, mimed astonishment, and patted the sides of her frock as if it had pockets. "I must have left them in my other cloak," she announced with her best innocent look.

I made my usual embarrassed attempt to hide behind her, but it never works—Ashleigh is six inches shorter than me.

Turkeyface frowned. "Where are your escorts?" he asked.

"Oh, they're around somewhere. They told us to meet them here," Ashleigh tried.

Our challenger grew sterner. "This event is for the Forefield community and their guests only," he said icily. "I'm afraid I can't admit you without a ticket or, at the very least, an escort."

Our wisest choice, I thought, would be to leave by the door and sneak back in through a window, crossing our fingers that the watchdog would keep his eye on the entrance rather than the room behind him. Well—our very wisest choice would be to go home, but I knew the Enthusiast would never agree to *that*.

"Can't we just—" she began.

"I'm afraid the rules on this point are very—" Turkeyface countered, speaking over her words.

I felt the blushing faintness so familiar from years of hanging out with Ashleigh. But as I tried to distract myself by wondering whether I had turned as red as Turkeyface, my ears caught a sound as welcome as a fire drill during finals week. It was a voice behind me speaking miraculous words: "It's all right, Mr. Waters. They're my guests."

Turning, I recognized the speaker as my Mysterious Stranger.

Turkeyface looked as astonished as I felt. "Really, Parr?" he said, raising an eyebrow. "Both of them? Two dates, all for you? My, my, you're quite the lothario."

Did my hero turn faintly pink himself, or was that an effect of the lighting? "No, just one—the other is Ned's guest—right, Ned?" He grabbed a square-set guy by the shoulder. "Got your tickets, Ned? Here, hand them over."

The boy called Ned fumbled in a vest pocket—he wore a vest!—and pulled out a clump of paper, a pack of cinnamon gum, a pencil stub, a tuning fork, and, finally, a pair of tickets. They appeared to be printed on smooth, thin cardboard like theater tickets, not Xeroxed onto colored paper like school notices. My hero contributed a pair of his own.

Turkeyface pushed his glasses down his nose to inspect the tickets. He made no further objections, however, waving us into the room and turning back to menace new arrivals.

Once we were out of his range, Ashleigh reached up and hugged the arm of the Mysterious Stranger called Parr. "Our hero," she cried. "You saved our lives! Without your aid, we would have been forced to climb in a window, endangering our Necks and Frocks. How can we ever thank you?"

"Hey, no problem," he answered. "Always glad to do what we can to foil old Wattles. Right, Ned?"

"The supreme joy of our young lives, foiling Wattles," agreed the one called Ned.

"Supreme though the joy of foiling Wattles may be, it can never compare in value to the service that you have rendered us tonight," argued Ash. "How will we ever repay you?"

"Honestly, we were happy to. But if you really want to thank us, some dances should do it," said Parr.

"With pleasure," cried Ashleigh. I inclined my head.

"And will you tell us the names of our dancing partners?" asked the handsome hero, turning to me.

I felt my blush intensify. With all the blood rushing to my cheeks, I worried that none would remain to carry oxygen to my vital organs. "I'm Julie—Julia Lefkowitz," I said, "and this is Ashleigh Rossi."

To my horror, Ashleigh curtsied. "And you, sir?" she asked.

"Charles Grandison Parr, at your service, madam," he said, sweeping an imaginary hat off his head and executing a bow worthy of Dodworth. "Allow me to introduce my companion, Edgar Downing, aka Ned the Noodle."

"Don't listen to old Granddad. Nobody calls me that," put in Ned, kicking at his friend.

"He's a dreamer, old Noodles. A fine intelligence, but a dreamer," countered Parr, dodging neatly.

"But what, pray, did Mr. Turkeyface have against us?" asked Ashleigh. "Did he think we were going to steal the ancestors off the wall?"

The suggestion seemed almost reasonable. The walls of the room in which we were standing—a sort of medieval hall, complete with suits of armor, presumably empty, guarding the doors at each end—were covered from ear-height to the rafters with paintings of sour-looking men in dark suits.

"Oh, I doubt it—that's just old Wattles acting wattly," said Parr. "Of course, there *was* the time the Emerson House seniors sneaked in the night before Founder's Day and turned all the pictures upside down. But I can't imagine he would blame *you* for that."

"Oh, yes he would, Gramps. He'd blame them for anything

that crossed his mind. They're girls, aren't they? He's a dirty-minded old Puritan. He probably thinks dancing is the devil's work," said Ned.

"But nobody's actually dancing," Ashleigh pointed out.

Indeed, the room was full of people milling around in knots like ours. Although a small chamber orchestra stationed overhead on a minstrels' balcony was pouring forth music, not a single couple was dancing to it. The young musicians were even pretty good too, if you like Mozart and can ignore acne.

"Everyone's waiting for the headmaster and his wife to open the dance. It's a Forefield tradition," said Parr. "But," he continued after a pause, "how did you wind up here without tickets? Did you lose them? Or do you actually have escorts who stood you up?"

When we hesitated, wondering how to answer, Ned added, "Don't tell me you really crashed! Somebody dared you, right? You can't have come of your own free will."

Ashleigh and I looked at each other, but before she could open her mouth, a fanfare sounded from the musicians' gallery. A hush fell across the grand hall. A tuxedoed teenage trumpeter put down his instrument and announced in a voice as brassy as the horn: "Ladies and gentlemen, please take your places for the Founder's Quadrille!"

In the bustle that followed, a silver-haired gentleman emerged from the crowd and led a stout but handsome lady to the far end of the room, by the empty knights. Couples, mostly older, arranged themselves geometrically down the grand hall. Music struck up, and the lead couple began the elegant ritual of walk, slide, and balancé as the others looked on.

Ashleigh took Parr by the arm. "Well, sir? Didn't you want to dance?" she cried.

"Yes, but we have a while. They always play one or two really weird antique dances before the waltzes. It takes at least an hour after that before they get to the normal stuff. We have a long wait ahead."

"But why wait—don't you know the quadrille?" persisted Ash.

"Well, *we* do—they teach us in phys. ed. when we're first formers—but I can't imagine *you* do. Unless—you're not from Miss Wharton's, are you?" Parr gave us a doubtful look.

"No, but we do know our quadrilles. Which one is this? The Coquette? The Polo? The Basket Dance? Well, we can wing it— I mean, we will endeavor to improvise. Come on, the rest of the couples are starting to dance!" said Ashleigh, stuffing her purse and wrap behind the nearest suit of armor. Parr let her pull him into position at the bottom of the room.

"Are you ready?" said Ned, turning to me. "I'm glad you showed up—for once I get someone good to dance with."

I tucked my things in beside Ashleigh's, took the arm he offered, and followed him off to join our friends.

∽

The Founder's Quadrille couldn't be more unlike twenty-first century dancing. Today, a couple or small group stands together, rhythmically contorting their arms, shoulders, torso, hips, and lower limbs. The point is to wiggle in harmony with one's companions while distinguishing oneself from the crowd by imaginatively displaying one's attractive parts, all the while avoiding—as far as possible—looking like a dork.

Not so the Founder's Quadrille. Looking like a dork seems to be required. Another difference is the miles that the quadrille dancers cover. They step forward and back, spin, approach the opposite corners, return to the first spot. Often throughout the dance, Ned took my hand, walked me and turned me, bowed to me and acknowledged my curtsy. But often, too, I found myself face-to-face with some other gentleman, or arm-in-arm with a lady. With all this to-ing and fro-ing, it was hard to carry on a conversation.

I fell to musing about the voice of my Mysterious Stranger, Charles Grandison Parr. In the six times I'd seen him before, I had never once heard him speak. Even at the Sports Barn, he had merely bowed in silence. His voice, now that I heard it, was nothing like what I had imagined: not a rumbling bass, but a strong, smooth tenor, full of caressing vowels that seemed to reach to my very toes and fingertips. It vibrated through me as he talked disjointedly with Ashleigh, leading her through the steps of the dance.

"You never answered Grandison, you know," said Ned, giving me his hand. "Why *did* you crash the dance?" Funny, he had the rattling bass voice I had imagined for Parr. Hearing it now, it seemed unsubtle. Why did I imagine Parr would sound like that?

The quadrille separated us for a minute, leaving me time to think. I decided to tell the truth—or part of it, at least.

"It was Ashleigh," I said as Ned and I slid to the right, then left. We were well matched as dancers—the same height, so that our eyes were exactly level. "Ash gets these ideas in her head. Last year it was marine biology, the year before it was candy making. There's no way to stop her, short of locking all the doors and windows from the outside."

The dance carried Ned to Ashleigh's corner, where he turned her by the arm; for a breathless moment I felt Parr's hand on my own arm and looked up into his eyes. Then Ned was back. "Ashleigh's amazing," he said. "I've never seen anyone dance the Founder's Quadrille with actual enthusiasm! Not that I've seen all that many people dance it," he added after a foray into opposite corners, during which I gave my hand not to my hero but to a middle-aged gentleman with a potbelly, from the next set of couples, "mostly just the older teachers and the girls from Miss Wharton's. And us, of course, when we can't avoid it."

"Sorry to put you through this," I said, feeling a little hurt.

"No, no, I didn't mean that," said Ned. "This is surprisingly fun." He grinned at me. "You're not so bad, for a girl."

The music drew to a close, and we made our bows and curtsies. As the four of us stood in an awkward square, wondering what to do next, the band struck up again. Hidden within what sounded like a waltz by Strauss was the tune to "Take It Back," by the Wet Blankets—a favorite of Ashleigh's for most of the summer, and not yet fully abandoned despite her new interests.

"Hey, Noodles, they're playing your tune!" said Parr.

"Oh, are you a Wet Blankets fan?" asked Ashleigh eagerly.

"Yeah, I pretty much like them a lot," Ned said.

"Don't be so modest," said Parr. "He wrote this arrangement. Ned's our school composer."

"Really? I *love* this song," cried Ashleigh.

"In that case, would you like to dance?" Ned asked her.

This time it was Parr's turn to ask me, "Shall we?" and offer his hand.

⟡

Once the two of us were alone together—that is, as alone as a pair can be in a room full of dancing couples—my hero seemed to lose his suave. As for me, I had been tongue-tied from the start. Standing beside the Magnet of My Yearning—touching his hand—frantically sending signals to my toes to keep them from tangling with his: none of this was likely to make me articulate. I worried that my nervousness had infected my partner.

The silence stretched out. Clearly one of us had to say something.

Parr began.

"Haven't I seen you around town before?"
"I think so—at least, I know I've noticed *you*."
"The Sports Barn, was it? Or the candy store?
Didn't I see you with Samantha Liu?"
"That's right. She says you know her brother, Zach.
Are you another black belt in Nintendo?"
"I only wish! I'm blue, three down from black—
that is, assuming you refer to kendo."
"Kendo! Right! Kendo! Well, I'm clearly not
a black belt in talking. At least, not tonight."
"Hey, don't you think it's getting kind of hot?
After this dance, you want to grab a bite?
They've got a bar set up by the parterre.
Just chips and soda, but it's cooler there."

I nodded my agreement and fell silent again, internally kicking myself for my comments. Would Parr realize I had stored up every sighting like a treasure in my heart? Uncool, uncool. And that Nintendo gaffe—what sort of marshmallow head would he take me for? Yet how handsome he looked as he was laughing at me! His smile crinkled his turquoise eyes and stamped a single dimple in his left cheek. And it *was* kind of him to change the subject and suggest going for food, as if he had sensed my discomfort. Or was he merely looking for an excuse to ditch me?

With these thoughts, I waltzed myself dizzy in his arms.

The dance ended, the couples pattered their applause, I retrieved my things from behind the armor, and Parr and I stepped out into the welcome coolness of the October night.

Chapter 6

More adders ∽ Ginger ale ∽ untimely Flushing ∽
we dance the Sir Roger de Coverly.

*A*re you imagining a romantic scene of distant music, softly scented breezes, and twinkly lanterns, with moonlight falling over everything? Do you picture me beginning to shiver, while Parr wraps me tenderly in my shawl? In your vision, does he leave his arms casually around me as we lean against the balustrade, gazing at the stars?

Happy dream!

It was crowded on the long brick terrace overlooking the parterre. (A parterre, in case you were wondering—I was—turns out to be a chessboard arrangement of flower beds.) Now past the season of prime bloom, the Forefield parterre minced down to a long lawn, which swooped down to the river. Staircases and gravel paths threaded the flower beds, punctuated by large stone urns spilling over with late grasses and vines.

On the terrace where we stood, boys in blazers, now and then with a date in a pale dress, jostled one another to get at the food and drinks. Spilled pretzels crunched underfoot. From time to time clumps of muttering youths burst into wild chortles, as if to celebrate some successful act of wickedness. Released from his guard table, Turkeyface stalked along the edge of the terrace, sniffing the air for illicit smoke.

Grandison Parr led me to a sheltered spot by a pair of planters. "What would you like to drink?" he asked.

"Hmm—ginger ale?" I hoped the choice wouldn't sound too babyish.

"Right. Be right back." He pushed his way into the crowd.

At first I kept his golden head in sight, but after he turned around and glanced at me twice, I looked away, embarrassed to be caught staring. When I looked again, he was gone.

A long time went by.

I played with the fringes of my wrap, braiding and unbraiding them.

I wondered whether Ashleigh was still dancing. I considered going to find her, but decided to stay put, in case Parr came back.

Three or four gangly boys nearby nudged and punched one another. They ejected one and gave him a little push in my direction. He approached hesitantly.

"So, um, you wanna dance?" he muttered, addressing an area a little below my collarbones. He couldn't have been more than fourteen.

"Sorry, I can't—I'm waiting for my . . . escort . . . to come back with a drink," I answered.

With a little gulping noise, the boy skittered back to the safety of his companions.

A girl in green leaned against my planter, glancing sideways at me. I considered speaking, but decided against it. The girl's escort soon appeared and carried her away to the ballroom.

A handsome guy with the look of a large and powerful cat—a junior, I thought, or possibly even a senior—presently took her place. He plucked a pair of cigarettes from his blazer pocket and held them out. "Trade you a smoke for a light," he offered.

I shook my head. "Sorry, I don't have any matches."

He tucked the cigarettes away and leaned against my planter, his arm touching mine. I edged away, but he relaxed closer to me, keeping his arm in contact with mine.

"Sounds like they're finally done with the ancient music," he said after a minute. "Let's go dance."

"I can't. I'm waiting for someone."

He raised an eyebrow. "You've been waiting a long time. Are you sure he's coming back?"

I hesitated, considering what to say. I was beginning to have doubts.

The cat-guy pressed his advantage. "You seem pretty bored. If you don't want to dance, I'm sure we can find other things to do." He raised the eyebrow even higher. A hundred years ago, I thought, would he have twirled a moustache instead? I gripped the planter behind me, wondering how to get rid of him.

To my relief, rescue came running up, in the form of the person ultimately responsible for my trouble: Ashleigh.

"There you are," she cried. She turned her head and called behind her, "See, I told you she'd still be here!"

Parr and Ned followed more slowly, their hands full of drinks they were trying not to spill.

"Sorry that took so long," said Parr. "They didn't have ginger ale at the bar. I had to try three different vending machines." With a flourish, he presented me with a cold can. Glad to have something to do with my hands, I busied myself with it, snapping it open and sipping; the bubbles got up my nose.

The feline guy gave me what I imagined he must consider an intimate look, then turned to the newcomers. "Hey, Parr, your

girlfriend here was about to give up on you," he said. "What?"
he added, "no drink for me?"

"Hello, Chris," said Parr coldly. "I hear Wattles is looking for
you. Oh, look—there he is now."

Indeed, Turkeyface appeared to be heading toward us.

The cat-guy brushed my arm with his hand. "Catch you
later," he said, and melted away in the opposite direction.

"Ig, who was *that*?" said Ashleigh.

"I don't know, W———, maybe?" I suggested, naming a se-
ductive creep in a Jane Austen novel.

"You don't know Chris? Chris Stevens?" said Parr. "He
looked as though he knew you pretty well—or wanted to, anyway." Parr paused, as if deciding whether to say more, then
added, "I hope he wasn't bothering you. I really am sorry I was
gone so long."

"Grand Parr is a stubborn old thing," rumbled Ned. "Ashleigh told him you'd be just as happy with Sprite or Coke, but he
wouldn't believe it. He had to drag us all the way out to the new
science library."

"I said I'd bring ginger ale," said Parr. "A promise is a promise. If I had known Chris would come sniffing around— Was he
being obnoxious?"

"Nothing terrible, just asking me to dance," I said.

"Sounds like a plan," said Ned. "The waltzes are finally over.
I mean, you waltz beautifully," he added hastily, addressing Ashleigh, "but now we won't be the only ones dancing . . . kids, I
mean, not teachers . . ." He trailed off.

"I'm up for it," I said, eager to leave my planter. Gulping
down ginger ale, I followed my companions back into the ballroom.

✎

On the dance floor, both the music and the crowd had increased in volume. A DJ had taken over from the band.

At first I felt more self-conscious than ever, dancing without the prescribed steps of the quadrille or waltz. There's something especially awkward about free-form wiggling in a ball gown, and to make matters worse, the Guy of My Dreams was watching. But the rhythm of the music quickly took over, and with it the release that comes from vigorous physical activity.

Dancing in a group of four was a far cry from quadrilling or waltzing in couples. For one thing, Parr no longer touched me (except the occasional accidental, electrical brush). It was too loud to talk, beyond a shouted word or two. Soon several friends of Parr and Ned's caught sight of Ashleigh and me and joined us.

After a number of songs I found myself at the center of a circle of guys, detached from my friend and our rescuers. The ginger ale began to make its presence known. I excused myself—hoping that the boys would have the guts to go on dancing without the presence of a girl to give them an excuse—and went off to find a ladies' room.

Ladies' rooms, it turns out, don't flourish in boys' schools. Each likely-looking door seemed to taunt me. I discovered a coat closet, a broom closet, a conservatory dripping with greenery, and wood-paneled, book-lined chambers of various shapes and sizes—but no restroom. At last I found a chaperone to ask. She directed me to a boys' bathroom, temporarily reassigned to meet the needs of female guests. "Boys: STOP! Girls: GO!" read a laser-printed sign taped to the door—not, I thought, the most tactful way to put it.

The uneasy sense of trespass that I'd felt all evening intensified when I went in. What most unnerved me were the urinals. With their exposed position, unprotected by so much as a doorless stall; with their long, jutting necks and their intense smell— of ammonia, strong detergent, and something else—is it any wonder I slunk past with a shudder?

I chose a stall at the end of the long room. As I sat resting my feet and watching the rows and columns of blue tiles dance a quadrille before my eyes, I heard the door swing open. I froze— boys?! No, thank God—girls. Just girls. Prep-school girls, judging by their accents. Perhaps girls from Miss Wharton's?

I decided to wait them out.

There seemed to be four or five of them. Some made for the toilet stalls while their friends stood by the sinks. A couple of them compared and exchanged lipsticks; another requested a comb. ("Promise you don't have nits?"—"Will you get over that? Fourth grade was six years ago!")

They praised each other's shoes and disparaged various boys, mostly unknown to me, although I did hear the name of Chris Stevens. "Unthinkable creep, keep him away from me!" commented one girl with a melodious voice that seemed to curl musically around my ears.

"Oh, I don't know, he has a sort of viscous charm," disagreed another.

"I *guess*, if you like a guy to *ooze* at you," answered her friend.

Their conversation went on for so long that the toilet seat began to dig uncomfortably into the upper half of my lower limbs. I was considering making a break for it when I heard another familiar name.

"Anyone at all? My choice, the whole school? Okay, give me Parr," said the curly-voiced anti-oozer.

"Grandison Parr? The junior—the fencer?"

"That's the one. Mmmm! Rich, firm goodness."

"Really? You've experienced this firsthand?"

"Oh, don't I wish! I'm not *that* lucky."

"Parr? Isn't he taken?" objected one of the urinators from her stall. "He seems to have a date, anyway. That tall—"

An ill-timed flush, echoing in the tiled, high-ceilinged room, cut off the rest of the sentence. Considering all the ill-timed flushing I'd been doing myself that evening, I reflected— flushing of the skin, not of the toilet—(the water gurgled to a stop before I could finish the thought; I turned my attention back to the deeply interesting conversation—)

"—and the little one in red? Where did they *come* from? Where did they *get* those *dresses?*"

"I think the tall one's his sister. She kind of looks like him. She was dancing more with that dorky guy, the one in the three-piece suit."

"No, but would you let your sister dance with the dorky guy in the three-piece suit?"

"Would you let your girlfriend?"

"Well, they were all in the same set, anyway, early on. Did you see the little red one bouncing away? No way she learned *that* from the quadrille sergeant!"

"The guy in the funny suit is Parr's roommate. I still think the girlfriend is the tall one. She—"

As if to mock me, the last urinator finished her business and drowned out the end of another interesting sentence. By the time her toilet ceased its gurgling, the girls had clattered out of bathroom, leaving me alone to stare dizzily at the blue tiles.

When I rejoined my party, Ned and Ashleigh were dancing vigorously to the last few bars of "Take It Back"—the Wet Blankets version, not Ned's waltz—while Parr looked on with an amused smile.

"There you are," he said. "I was afraid I'd lost you again."

"It took me a while to find the ladies' room. They hid it behind a sort of greenhouse thing and a room full of silver cups in glass cases."

"Oh, you found the trophy room? Good place to take a nap when you're supposed to be in study hall. There's a big, puffy sofa behind the cabinets, and nobody ever goes in there."

The song ended, and the trumpeter blew a fanfare. I saw that the band had reassembled in the musicians' gallery. The room fell silent. Parr leaned close so he could whisper in my ear, "I'm sorry to say this is it—the last dance." His breath tickled my neck. The sensation made me my heart pound so loudly, I was afraid he'd hear it.

"Ladies and gentlemen, please take your places for the Virginia reel!" announced the trumpeter to moans and cries of "Already?!" In Jane Austen's time—or her novels, at any rate—this dance, known to Miss Austen and her characters as the Sir Roger de Coverly, signals the end of a ball.

"I guess it's over," I said to Ashleigh. "Better call Zach."

"Zach?" asked Ned.

"Our ride home," I explained.

Ashleigh retrieved her purse from behind the knight, fished out her cell phone, and handed it to me. "Here, you do it—just hit redial," she said, grabbing Parr's arm. Ned offered me his again.

The Sir Roger de Coverly is a complicated and vigorous dance: no easy thing to get through while talking on a cell phone. Still, I managed somehow, and by the time the dance brought my friend and me back within talking distance, I was able to report that Zach was on his way.

Chapter 7

An unglass slipper ⌒ A Farewell to Forefield ⌒
I eat the Pancakes of Anguish.

The boys insisted on walking us to the gate, where we had told Zach to meet us. Clumsy in my silver pumps, I stumbled going down the steps. My right shoe flew off. Parr caught me by the elbow. "Careful, Cinderella," he said, retrieving the shoe. I stretched out my hand for it, but he held it back for a moment. "Should I keep this, in case I need to find you again?" he said.

"If you do, you'll have to carry me to my pumpkin."

"Don't tempt me," he said. Kneeling, he held the shoe in front of my foot. I couldn't decide which he was more like: a knight in a fairy tale, or an old-fashioned shoe salesman—the kind your grandmother might have taken you to when you were little, who measured your feet with a cold metal sliding device.

The knight, I decided. The salesmen, I remembered, always had a bald patch clearly visible from above; Parr's hair shone thick and pale in the moonlight.

Parr eased my shoe over my heel with a little wiggle. He rose and took my arm again, holding me steady as I picked my way downhill along the grassy edge of the road. We caught up with Ash and Ned, who were chattering about which Wet Blankets songs would make the best waltzes.

The rest of the walk went by in an instant. "Gentlemen, we cannot thank you enough for your gallantry," said Ashleigh when we reached the stone lions.

"Hey, it was our pleasure. Next time, though, don't give Wattles the satisfaction of gobbling at you—call first or drop an e-, and I'll make sure you get official invites," said Parr. "Here—got a pen, Noodles?"

Ned selected a small felt-tip pen from the items in his pocket.

"Paper?" asked Parr, fishing around in his own pockets.

"Here," said Ashleigh, thrusting her hand into his. "Write on my palm. I always do."

Zach drove up as Parr bent over Ashleigh's hand. "Oho! Grandison Parr!" he said, leaning over to pop open the passenger-side door. "So that's how it is, is it? Are you treating my little friends right?"

"Little friends, indeed!" said Ashleigh, waving her hand to dry the ink and flouncing into the car. "Mr. Parr is treating us with a great deal more respect than *you* do, Mr. Liu. He and Mr. Downing rescued us from a particularly nasty adder and stood up with us for a quadrille, a waltz, and the Roger de Coverly. He is entirely a gentleman."

"Yeah? Glad to hear it, because that's one ass I'd rather not have to kick. I'm not saying I *couldn't*, but it would be a challenge. Black belt yet, Parr?"

"No, don't worry, you're still king of the hill," said Parr. "I'm glad to see the Hunkajunk is still in one piece," he added. "But if you're so worried about the girls' safety, why are you driving them around in that thing?"

I was astonished to hear him speak that way about Zach's pride and joy. Last year Haichang Liu had passed on to his son the family's old—or, as Zach prefers to call it, *vintage*—Saab, as an early graduation present when Zach got into Cornell. Zach spent so much time tweaking, tuning, and polishing it that I was surprised he had managed to graduate afterward.

But Zach just laughed. "Jealous? Learn discipline, young lion, and someday you too may be worthy of such a car. Come on, Julie, get in."

"Hai, Sensei," said Parr, giving a little martial-arts bow, palms together. He opened the car door, helped me in, and handed me the end of my wrap, which was trailing out.

"Thanks so much for everything," I told him. "You too, Ned."

"No, thank *you*," said Ned, poking his head in Ashleigh's window. "I never dreamed I'd actually enjoy the Founder's Quadrille. I'm glad you two decided to crash."

"Me too," said Parr. "But once is enough for one evening. Don't let Zach wrap you around a tree—use that e-mail address to let us know you're okay, would you? Cparr@forefield.org."

"Yeah, yeah, get going before I wrap *you* around a tree," said Zach.

Parr shut the door and gave the car's rear end a little pat, like a cowboy with his horse, to send us on our way.

～

"So you know Grandison Parr?" asked Ashleigh.

Zach nodded. "He's a smartass, but a pretty fair swordsman. Decent guy on the whole. More than decent, actually—he helped me push the Saab all the way uphill to the garage when she broke down near the dojo last summer. Of course, he thinks that gives him the right to call her the Hunkajunk. Smartass. But he seems to like *you*." He gave Ashleigh a penetrating look.

"How long have the two of you been acquainted?" she asked.

"Oh, three or four years, I guess."

"How did you meet?"

"He practices kendo at the dojo."

"How could he? I was under the impression that the Forefield authorities kept their students locked up on the hill," said Ashleigh.

"No, they let them out for things like that. Haven't you ever seen them rowing on the river or riding around on horses in those ridiculous outfits? Besides, his family has a weekend house not all that far north, so he's around for part of the summer."

So that was why I'd seen him in town before school was in session.

"Are there any girls at the dojo?" asked Ashleigh.

"A few. Not as many as the guys, but a couple of the teachers are women, and there's a women's self-defense class that's pretty popular. Some of the karate classes have a fair number of girls in them. Why?"

"I was thinking kendo might be fun."

I was surprised to hear it. Didn't she realize that the martial arts uniform consisted of a short, bathrobelike tunic over loose trousers? How did she expect to kick an assailant without displaying her lower limbs? Was it too much to hope that we might be in for a craze change already?

"I think aikido would be more your thing," said Zach. "It's all about turning your enemy's strength against him, so your size doesn't matter so much, and face it, you're pretty little—in most ways, anyway. The main thing is balance and discipline."

Balance and discipline, I reflected, were not chief among Ashleigh's virtues. However, the conversation having left the riveting topic of Grandison Parr, it soon ceased to hold my attention;

for the rest of the brief ride home I stared out the window at the dark trees, reliving the hours just past and musing on the uncertain future.

⤴

The next morning—Saturday—I awoke to feel bouncing near my toes. I opened my eyes in wonder. Ashleigh, and so early! I could count on one hand the times she had willingly gotten up before me—and two of those times she had forgotten to turn back the clock for daylight saving time. Her enthusiasm must have reached quite a peak.

"There! Admit it. Was I not right to insist on our attending the dance? Did I not tell you that you would meet your Bingley and I my Darcy? Was he not *wonderful?* His charm, his gallantry! Come on, get up! Let's go give Samantha back her handbags and see if Zach's still there. Maybe he can tell me more about Darcy."

"Okay, okay. Ouch! I'm coming, you don't have to pull my feet off," I said. I was a little surprised to hear Ashleigh refer to Ned as Mr. Darcy. The square-set young composer seemed sweet enough, but nothing like the proud, aristocratic, icy-fiery hero of *Pride and Prejudice.* Nor did tall, teasing Parr seem in the least like the insipidly agreeable Mr. Bingley. And why should Zach be able to tell us anything about Ned, when Parr was the one he knew? I attributed Ashleigh's confusion to Love. The tender passion is not known for sharpening the intellect.

I packed up some schoolbooks and a favorite sweater—I was spending the rest of the weekend at my father's—and wheeled out my bike. Ashleigh rode beside me, chattering swoonily about the dances, the dresses, the music, the ballroom, and—most of all—the gentlemen. Mr. Darcy, she maintained, was the picture of perfection, although she generously allowed "my" Mr. Bingley to be an intelligent, lively, pleasant fellow. I smiled to myself at the thought of anyone preferring Ned to Parr, although certainly he—Ned, that is—seemed made for Ashleigh, with his musical enthusiasm and pocketful of peculiar objects. They even looked a little like each other, with the same curly hair and warm brown eyes.

When we reached the Lius', the doctors were planting bulbs in their garden. "Hello, girls," said Lily. "Samantha's in the kitchen. We just finished eating pancakes, but there's some batter left—you can have it if you're hungry."

"Mmmm! Thanks, Dr. Lily," I said.

"You better cook it first," said Haichang.

"You don't think pancake batter would make a good drink?" I asked.

"Is Zach around?" asked Ashleigh.

"He must be," I said. "The Saab's here."

"He's still sleeping, the lazybones," said Lily. "Serve him right if you eat up his pancakes. Go on, before the griddle cools down."

Sam was putting the butter away in the fridge, but she gladly took it out again when she saw us. She spooned batter onto the griddle.

"How was the boy hunt?" she asked. "Zach says you landed a couple of live ones."

"We did indeed have the good fortune to make the acquaintance of two young gentlemen of high character and pleasing appearance," said Ashleigh.

"Hmm, not quite how Zach put it. What about you, Julie? Did you have a good time? Meet any lofty and pleasing gentlemen?" asked Samantha.

"As a matter of fact, except for the really embarrassing parts, it was surprisingly fun. The guys we met were really nice—one of them was that friend of Zach's you and I ran into in the Sports Barn. I overheard some of the girls making fun of our dresses in the bathroom, but none of the guys seemed to mind how we looked. Lots of them danced with us, anyway. On the whole, it was one of the more successful of Ashleigh's marshmallow-headed schemes."

Ashleigh gave me her Reproachful Look. "You met Grandison Parr before?" she cried. "Why did you not tell me?"

"Oh—I—There wasn't much to tell. We just passed him at the mall—he didn't even talk to us, and Sam couldn't remember his name."

"Oh, that guy? I like him," said Sam. "But be careful. If this were a real Jane Austen story, one of those guys would turn out to be a cad who's only after your money."

"Scratch that—for me, anyway," I said.

"Or your honor, maybe—or just your clothes—remember that movie *Clueless*?" added Sam.

"Yes, well, if this were *Clueless*, we'd all fall in love with Zach," said Ashleigh scornfully, flipping the pancakes.

The person in question chose that moment to make his appearance in the kitchen, clad only in pajama bottoms and looking pleased with himself. Zach obviously shares the widespread opinion that his shirtless torso is a magnificent sight.

"Good plan! I wish you would. Then you'd be nice and give me those," he said, reaching for the pancakes with a fork.

Ashleigh fended him off with her spatula. "Keep your fork to yourself," she cried.

"I bet if I were *Grandison Parr* you'd let me have them. No, more than that—you'd make me my own batch. In heart shapes," said Zach, easily evading her spatula like the fencer he was. He skewered a pancake and crammed it into his mouth, then followed it with a chaser of syrup, drizzled directly from the bottle, which he held a few inches above his lips.

Ash jittered with indignation. "If you were Grandison Parr, you would never rob a defenseless female in this manner! You villain! You unspeakable adder! You are not fit to speak the name of the noble Mr. Darcy!"

Busy as I was admiring Zach's syrup caper, it took me a moment to realize what Ashleigh had said. As soon as I did, an electric shock went through me.

"Darcy," I gasped weakly. "Darcy—Parr?"

I bit my tongue to stop myself from revealing any more of my feelings before I had a chance to understand them myself. It was too late, however. Every eye was upon me.

"Why, yes, of course, Parr! Who did you think?" said Ashleigh. "Ned? Ned the Noodle—you thought *he* was Mr. Darcy?"

"No, of course not, don't be silly," I protested. "Frankly, neither of them seems much like Darcy to me."

"Really? You certainly didn't say so earlier this morning. I seem to recall you agreeing with me when I asserted that Darcy was wonderful. Are you not protesting just a teeny, tiny bit too much? Methinks?"

Zach took up the cry. "Look, she's blushing! Oho! Sensible Julie isn't so sensible today, is she, now? Who would have thought those Foreskin boys would break *two* hearts!"

"Stop it, you guys! I mean it! Ig—Ned—emphatic ig! I *really* don't like him. I mean, I like him fine, but I don't *like* him."

In my agony, it seemed, I had turned into a second grader.

Ashleigh gave me a look of happy condescension. "Now, now, my dearest Julia, I cannot see why you refuse to admit it. Ned is a very agreeable fellow indeed—almost as handsome as my Parr. The two of you are a perfect match, exactly the same height. And he likes you, Julie—you know he does. He danced the last dance with you, and the first dance. He tried to talk Parr into bringing you a Sprite instead of a ginger ale, so we could get back to you. And he even asked me for your e-mail address— well, he asked for both of our addresses, but I gave him yours. I could tell that was what he really wanted."

Could she be right? Could Ned have developed feelings for me like mine for Parr?

Samantha saw my discomfort and tried to help by turning the conversation from my affairs to Ashleigh's. "*Your* Parr? Are you admitting *you're* in love?"

Alas, Ashleigh's answer pained me more than all the previous conversation.

"In love?" said Ashleigh. "How can I answer *that*? If you believe—like our English instructress, Miss Nettleton—that true love comes only to those who, upon first meeting, speak together in rhyme and meter, so that their conversation produces a sonnet, then no. But I confess that never before have I encountered so gallant, so courageous, so handsome a gentleman as Grandison Parr. If ever there was a man born to capture my heart, then that man is Grandison Parr. And although modesty warns me to discount them, I believe I saw signs that he returned my regard. He danced the quadrille with me. He drew me apart from the others as he searched the campus from end to end for ginger ale, thus affording us quiet time together, accompanied only by Ned. He queried me most particularly about my childhood, my abode, and the society I keep, showing a keen interest in all my doings. And he took my hand in his to write his e-mail address on my palm—writing I preserve to this day, and will as long as hygiene permits it!" She held her hand up triumphantly, palm out.

"Yup, I saw that part," agreed Zach. "Well, aren't you the lucky girl! Won't you please, please give me another pancake? Surely I deserve a booby prize."

She shot him a look of scorn and handed the pancakes to me instead. But although I tried to eat as if nothing had happened, they stuck in my throat. As soon as I could, I escaped to my father's house to brood over my troubles.

Chapter 8

I Renounce my Dream ∽ I maintain my Dignity ∽
I carry boxes ∽ I E-mail.

Was Ashleigh right? Had Grandison Parr, over the course of the previous evening, developed feelings for Ashleigh?

There could be no doubt about *her* feelings for *him*. I knew that enthusiastic gleam in her eye all too well. Had I been deluding myself, daring to imagine that he might like *me*? Sitting on the bed in the room I shared with Amy's sewing machine, I went over the events of the previous evening in my mind, just as I had through the night. What a difference there was this time! Every clue that had raised my hopes could equally well dash them.

At first, Parr's promptness in rescuing us from the turkey-faced doorkeeper had seemed like evidence that my hero had noticed me, and maybe even liked me. But was that just wishful thinking? Wouldn't the gallant fencer have sprung to the aid of anyone in distress? Or maybe—I shuddered at the thought, then shuddered at myself for shuddering—maybe it was Ashleigh's daring and charm that had persuaded him to help us. After all, her liveliness, along with her rapidly developing maturity of looks, seemed to appeal to guys—especially in that crimson dress. Even Zach had noticed it. Why not Parr?

Then, Parr danced the first quadrille with her. I had put that down to her energy—she had pulled him onto the dance floor. But he certainly hadn't tried to resist, and they seemed to be enjoying it, chatting away. When he and I waltzed, our conversation seemed stilted and awkward. (Remembering the waltz, I felt his hand once again on my mind's waist and shivered with pleasure and distress.) The night before, when I looked back on our first conversation, I hoped its awkwardness might be due to our mutual attraction. Maybe he felt shy with me at first, just as I felt with him. But maybe not—maybe he merely found me dull.

Nobody could ever find Ashleigh dull.

Then there was Parr's long disappearance during the ginger-ale quest. At the time, I wondered whether he had been trying to abandon me entirely, but when he showed up with the elusive soft drink, I was touched. What a lot of trouble he'd taken for me, I thought. Now, though, Ashleigh's theory seemed equally likely: that he was trying to spin out his time with her.

The other apparent signs of Parr's feelings toward me—his friendly teasing, his disapproval when creepy Chris got too close, and his Cinderella remarks, which put him in the role of the prince—also melted away on closer inspection. I bit my lip to keep from crying with jealousy. Why did Ashleigh always get *everything*? Not only had she taken over my enthusiasm for Jane Austen, but now she seemed hell-bent on stealing my secret love!

For a long time I struggled with myself, feeling bitter resentment and condemning myself for it. After all, I could not question Ashleigh's generosity or the purity of her motives. When she fell for Parr, she had no idea that I had gotten there first. You could even say the whole thing was my own fault for not taking her into my confidence from the start. Ash would never have looked twice at a boy she knew I liked. She was too loyal. For my sake, she had even given up her plans to become a nun at age eight, when she learned that Jewish girls couldn't enter a Catholic sisterhood. If she had known my feelings, I believed she would have tried to suppress her own.

No, if somebody had to suppress her feelings, it should be me. After all, I was much better at it than Ashleigh. I would prove to myself, if it killed me, that I could be as generous as my friend.

Still, if Parr didn't see me in a romantic light, it didn't necessarily follow that he had chosen Ashleigh. She and I were far from the only ones who admired the handsome fencer. I remembered the Wharton girl in the bathroom with the crush on Parr. She considered him beyond her reach. She thought he was already taken. Well, perhaps he was—not by me or Ashleigh, as she seemed to assume, but by someone else!

And even if Parr's heart *was* free, did Ash or I stand a chance with him? Impossible to say. For, as I gradually realized, he was stuck in Forefield, and we would have no chance to get to know him better.

Hopeless, hopeless, all of it. The world that had seemed so bright and sharp faded to gray. Even the leaves blazing outside the window looked washed out, as if fall no longer mattered. I lay back on the bed, closed my eyes, and let tears leak into my ears.

❧

"Jul—Oh, napping?" said my stepmother disapprovingly, coming into the room with a perfunctory knock. "Would you mind

helping me downstairs, sweetie? I'm not supposed to lift anything."

I awarded myself half a dozen imaginary dollars: one for not
answering snappishly that Amy had interrupted a period of
quiet, mindful contemplation; two more for not telling her she
could perfectly well carry her own groceries; and the rest for not
smashing the furniture in my despair.

I spent the afternoon stowing bulk packages of toilet paper,
diet soda, and other scintillating commodities in the laundry
room and hauling junk from the other basement room up to the
attic. Although I didn't have the emotional strength to ask what
it all meant, I hoped the I.A. was preparing a new home for her
sewing machine, so I wouldn't have to live with it in my room.
She had been using it quite a bit over the last few weeks; the table
next to it was covered with pastel-colored fabric scraps.

I worked obediently, the physical activity distracting and
soothing me. Still, my sorrow preyed on my mind, killing any
urge to socialize; when Ashleigh called on Sunday, I even let
Amy tell her I was too busy to talk.

It wasn't until Monday evening—Columbus Day—that I
summoned the strength to check my e-mail. I found this message waiting:

From: Downing, Ned <edowning@forefield.org>
To: Julielefk@hotmail.com
Sent: Sunday, 2:21 P.M.
Subject: upsidedown headmasters

hi julie,
    hey it was fun dancign with you and ashley. if you guys snuck
into the great hall and turned the headmasters upside down would

that make them feetmasters? if you hung them on teh stairs would they be stairmasters? i hope you'll come help i have a plan but i'm not sure it'll work. pleaes say hi to ashley for me. do you have her email address?

best wishes

ned

Oh, great, I thought. The first time a boy ever invites me to hang out with him (or, more precisely, hang pictures with him), it's (a) the wrong boy, who (b) can't type, and (c) has the world's least romantic ulterior motive—a practical joke.

For a painful minute I considered going along with his plan, whatever it was: since it would have to take place on the Forefield campus, there was a chance I would see Parr again. But such pleasures, I told myself sternly, were not for me.

How, then, should I answer Ned's message? Sending him Ashleigh's e-mail address could only lead to more excruciating escapades. Given half a chance, the Enthusiast would surely insist on flipping the portraits, not only from her love of mischief, but from the same motive I was resisting: the hope of seeing Parr. However, it seemed cruel not to respond to Ned at all—what if I was right that he had fallen for Ash? And if he had, I caught myself thinking, perhaps he could win her away from Parr, leaving the field open for me. Hastily I squelched the thought.

After some hesitation, I wrote back:

Hi Ned,

Thank you for your message. I had a great time at the dance too. Overturning the Forefield headmasters sounds a little beyond me, though. Ashleigh might be up for it—but please don't let her

get mauled to death by fierce turkeys!!!! Her address is
sirashleigh@hotmail.com. (Remember to spell her name with an
eigh, or it won't get there.)

I added, "Please give my regards to Parr," deleted it, undeleted
it, deleted it again and added, "Hi to Parr," deleted and undeleted
that a few times, reinstated "Please give my regards to Parr,"
signed the message, and hit <send>.

By Tuesday morning, while no more cheerful, I was at least
calm enough to meet Ashleigh and pretend things were normal.
Our first chance to speak came during lunch. "There you are,"
she said excitedly, slipping into the seat next to me. "Why didn't
you call me back? Didn't Amy give you my message?"

"What message?" I lied.

"Oh, that certified public adder! Of course she wouldn't give
you my message, even though I told her it was important. I was
calling to say I received an e-mail from Him."

"Him who—Ned?"

"Ned! Faugh! How your mind does run on Ned! From Parr,
of course."

My sandwich—one of Amy's ordinarily delicious pesto-and-
roasted-vegetable specials—turned to leaf mold in my mouth.

"Really? What did he have to say?"

"He was glad we reached home in safety—I e-mailed him
right away, as he had requested. He described his experience with
kendo and recommended it as a sport well suited to an active
young lady. He passed along greetings from several of the gentlemen with whom we danced. He also praised my dancing—he
said he had enjoyed my 'unique approach to the quadrille.' What
do you think it means? Do you think he *likes* me?"

On the whole, I did tend to think so. Yet I feared that in her enthusiasm Ashleigh might have mistaken a mild regard for a more intense emotion.

Or did I merely *hope* so?

"Sounds like it might be a good sign," I said cautiously.

"Doesn't it? I really think it is. Oh," added Ash, "and he said to tell you hi."

Yvette and Yolanda joined us, and the conversation turned to more general topics, such as the impossibility of getting parts in the school production of *West Side Story* when competing against people like Michelle Jeffries and Cordelia Nixon, who ran the show like a popularity contest.

After school Ashleigh wanted to delve deeper into the subtleties of Parr's message, but I begged off, pleading homework. I hurried to my father's house. For once the I.A. was in a subdued, even glum mood that matched my own, and she left me alone. For several hours I balanced chemical equations, memorized French verbs, and tried to anticipate Ms. Nettleton's opinion on the death of Romeo's cousin Tybalt. When it came to history, however—a chapter on European weapons and military strategy in the Middle Ages—I couldn't concentrate. The subject reminded me too much of Ashleigh and Parr.

I checked my e-mail again, and there it was:

From: Parr, Grandison <cparr@forefield.org>
To: julielefk@hotmail.com
Sent: Tuesday, 9:45 P.M.
Subject: Help me stop them

Dear Julia,
Your friend Ashleigh gave me your e-mail address—I hope that's okay?

I was relieved to hear that Zach Liu got you home in one piece. Or I guess I should say two pieces, since there are two of you.

I take it all the shoes arrived safely too?

Which brings me to the topic of this message: safety.

I assume Ashleigh told you about the plan she and Ned are cooking up to rearrange the portraits in the Great Hall. Is there any way you can talk her out of it? Ned's already in trouble for miking the stalls in the faculty bathroom and wiring them to the PA system. Wattles has it in for him. I'm worried that if Ned goes through with the portrait thing, he could lose his scholarship.

I tried to talk him out of it, but he says he doesn't want to disappoint Ashleigh. Can you stop her? She's obviously strong willed and high-spirited, but you seem like a sensible person, someone she might listen to.

I'm glad you came to the dance last weekend. I've never had such a good time at a Forefield social event. I wouldn't have thought it was possible. If only you'd crash our classes, I'd even look forward to trigonometry.

Sincerely yours,

C. Grandison Parr

My pulse beat hard in my throat as I read this message, especially the last paragraph. He was glad I had come to the dance! He'd look forward to trig if I were there! The first two times I read the message, I hardly took in the main subject, Ashleigh and Ned's dangerous plan.

The third time through, however, I was struck by a painful thought: In English, *you* can be plural as well as singular. Perhaps Parr meant that he was glad to have danced with me *and Ashleigh*—that the presence of me *and Ashleigh* would make trig bearable. After all, that was how he used *you* in the second sentence, the one about Zach getting us home in two pieces. And Ash was the topic of the message, its entire purpose. Probably the *you* in question included me only as an afterthought: probably it was meant to express more strongly Parr's admiration for my lively friend, whom he had already praised.

To him, I was nothing but a sensible person.

All right, then, Julia Lefkowitz, I told myself: BE sensible.

Dear Grandison,

I wish I could help, I really do. But in the 10 years I've known Ashleigh, I've only been able to talk her out of one scheme—the time she wanted to jump off the roof wearing papier-mâché wings. I convinced her to try it with her doll first. After Arabella's (the doll's) head cracked open, Ash didn't speak to me for a week and a half. The first thing she said to me afterward was that she'd never listen to me again. And she pretty much never has.

Did you try to talk her out of the plan yourself? I think she'd be more likely to listen to you than to me. I know she admires and respects you.

Or maybe you could somehow get Wattles to lock the hall extra carefully for a while?

I'm sorry I can't help more, especially since Ash and I owe you so much for saving us from Wattles last week.

Sincerely yours,

Julia Lefkowitz

I read the message through, deleted the sentence about Ashleigh admiring Parr for fear it might be betraying her trust (or, muttered a little voice inside me, for fear it might give him ideas), and clicked <send>.

Chapter 9

Rumors of rivals ∽ I withdraw ∽ I join up ∽ a Surprising communication from my Mother ∽ a Shocking communication from my Stepmother ∽ Ashleigh too ∽ I Endeavor to come to my Senses.

Have you ever tried to avoid your best friend: the girl who knows all your secrets (or all but *one*), the girl who up to now has spent every free moment by your side and is liable to appear at your window at any hour of the day or night with acorns in her hair, expecting to be admitted?

If so, you know how difficult the days that followed were for me.

Ashleigh wanted me to read and interpret all her e-mail messages from Parr—and there were a ton of them. She never tired of combing through them for clues to his feelings, or of dreaming up schemes to see him in person.

"Julia! Come read this—I need your advice," she said one afternoon as I sat on her bed doing my math homework.

"What is it?"

"A disturbing message indeed. I need your help interpreting it."

"Is it another e-mail from Parr? I don't know, Ash, aren't those sort of private?"

"My dearest Julia! You know I have no secrets from you! Anyway, it's from Samantha Liu."

"Oh, okay," I said. Looking over her shoulder at her computer screen, I read:

Hi Ashleigh—

I asked around for you; see below. Look how you're ruining my reputation! I'll let you know if I hear anything else.

—Sam

> Oh, so your "friend" wants to know about Grandison Parr, does
> she? Really, Sam, I wouldn't have thought he'd be your type—
> isn't he a little romantic for you? I mean, he writes *poetry*!
> Well, you're in good company, according to my sources at Miss
> Wharton's. He's—what's that thing they all chase after in
> Quidditch? The Golden Snitch? Unfortunately, they say he's
> going out with a tall blonde. I haven't been able to pinpoint
> which one, but it might be Emily Wardwell or Kayla Thwaite—
> they were both seen with him at the recent Forefield dance.
> Sorry! But don't despair. I'd back you against any Wart, no
> matter how tall and blonde. Do I get a reward for this? Maybe
> you could get me a date with that yummy brother
> of yours?
> Just kidding, sort of . . .

"Well?" I said.

"Well, what do you think?" said Ashleigh. "Do you think it's true?"

"I don't know, Ash. What do *you* think?" I selfishly hoped it was. I would far rather have a Wart girl as a rival than my beloved Ashleigh. Maybe then Ash and I could even share a companionable gloom.

But Ashleigh quickly cheered herself up: her enthusiasm

comes with a hearty dose of optimism. "I don't know!" she said. "My impulse is to believe Miss Liu, whose judgment is remarkably sound. However, we have no information about her friend's judgment—we don't even know who her friend *is*. It's just like Samantha to be so discreet! Perhaps those 'sources' may be mistaken. Parr's last message sounded very encouraging. Listen to this: 'Sounds like you and Julia had a great time apple picking last weekend. I wish I'd been there.' What do you think that means? Do you think he *likes* me?"

These discussions made me so miserable that I tried my best to avoid them, and when I found that impossible, I began to avoid Ashleigh.

At least one good thing came from her devotion to Parr: she agreed to give up the plan to monkey with the headmasters. I heard this first in an e-mail from Ned, who blamed me for her change of heart. Later Parr made the same mistake and thanked me. I answered Ned politely but briefly, and Parr not at all, although I found it hard to keep my cursor away from the <send> button. I couldn't let myself carry on a correspondence, however innocent, with Ashleigh's beloved. After a few unanswered messages, Parr stopped writing.

I threw myself into my schoolwork, the best way I knew to numb my mind. I took dawn bike rides and hikes in the hills among the ever-barer trees, sneaking out while Ash was still in bed. I spent long hours working in the storeroom and on the computer, attempting to straighten out the inventory and accounts of Helen's Treasures. And holding my inner nose, I joined the staff—or, as Ms. Nettleton called it, the *crew*—of *Sailing to Byzantium*, our high school literary magazine.

The Nettle gave me the position of assistant editor and began smiling at me in class. My father was overjoyed. He rained down little pellets of smugness, like a squirrel shelling nuts overhead. "I'm glad you've started taking a real interest in your academic career," he beamed. "Amy will be so proud."

When Ashleigh expressed her astonishment at my extracurricular activity, I lied to her (a painful new habit), explaining that Dad had threatened to withhold my allowance unless I joined up. She generously offered to keep me company, but I told her it would only make the whole thing worse if she suffered too.

Even without her, I suffered. The worst was the loneliness. Though surrounded by people, I felt utterly isolated. I missed my friend, the only person who really understood me, yet in her company I felt lonelier than ever.

◦∕◦

Early one evening, as I sat on my bed staring out the window at the pattern made by the oak branches—a lattice of bars between me and heaven—I heard a knock at my door.

"You in there, honey?" asked my mother.

"Uh-huh—come in."

"It's so dark in here! Why don't you turn on a light? No, leave it if you like this better—listen, I want to talk to you." She sat down on the end of my bed and curled her legs under her. "I've noticed that you haven't been yourself for the last few weeks, and I think I know why."

"You do?" I said. Had my secret somehow gotten out? A tingling alarm swept over me, accompanied by a soft cascade of relief, as if something tight had loosened. I felt tears well up in my eyes.

Mom put her arms around me and stroked my hair. "I'm

sorry, honeybear. I'm so sorry. I know it's been tough on you with your father gone and money being tight. You take it so hard—you're such a grown-up kid. But it's not your job to take care of everything. That's up to me, I'm the mom here. And honey, I promise you it will all be all right. I'm not going to let us starve. And I'm not going to stay dependent on your father, either. I realize Helen's Treasures isn't working out the way I hoped, so I've been looking for a job. No, just listen. I've had a few offers I could have taken, but I held off because I was waiting to hear from the one I really want, teaching art. But even if I don't get it, there are other things I can do, so you don't have to take everything on your big little grown-up freckled shoulders. Okay, honey? Shh, shh—there, there. Better now? I was going to wait to tell you until I heard about this job for sure, but you've seemed so stressed that I thought I'd better talk to you now."

As she spoke, I felt the relief and tension swirl around within me, trading places like a couple in a quadrille. My secret was safe! A reprieve!—yet a disappointment too, to find myself once again deeply alone.

I wiped my eyes and pulled myself together. "That's great, Mom," I said.

ﾟ✑

Next it was Amy's turn. On Tuesday she cornered me behind the sewing machine, where I was doing my math homework. "I know why you've been so sad lately, sweetie, and I'm touched, I really am," she said. "I know how disappointed you must be after all these years alone, and especially with all the help you've been giving me getting the room ready. I wish I had good news for you now. But I promise, your father and I are doing everything we can, and I'm sure we'll be successful sooner or later."

"You are?" I asked, not sure what she was talking about. I had a strong hunch it wasn't anything good, though.

"Oh, yes, we're doing everything we can. After we lost the baby, we went to see a new fertility specialist in New York who has an excellent track record with couples in our situation."

I stared at her. What was she talking about? What baby?

"We've been following his instructions carefully—which, I must say, we've both enjoyed," she continued, with a coy smirk that made my stomach lurch. "And on the plus side, at least until I get pregnant again, I can help you carry your things down to your new room in the basement. Have you chosen what color you want yet? I thought I'd paint this room a nice pastel yellow, since we don't know whether it'll be a boy or a girl. I always think yellow goes with everything. What do you say, should we stencil a border of ducks just under the ceiling, so your little brother or sister will have something to look at? Or stars on the ceiling?"

For a long time I was speechless. The I.A. didn't notice—she was too busy planning where she would put the changing table and the bassinet. To lose in one stroke my status as an Only Child and my airy (if sewing-machine-ridden) bedroom! To be banished to the basement! So that was why she'd been empty-ing out that dark little room downstairs—not to hide away her sewing machine, but to hide away *me*!

And what could my father possibly want with another child, when he hardly bothered to talk to the one he already had?

೨

Ashleigh caught me Thursday morning as I was exiting the win-dow for an early run. "Hang on, Jules," she said, climbing down to meet me at the tree's roots. "I need to talk to you." (Oh, no, I thought, Ashleigh too!) "Is something the matter?" she asked. "Are you okay? I almost get the feeling you've been avoiding me. Did I do something wrong? Is there any way I can make it better?"

I was overcome with guilt. My best friend had taken the trouble to get out of bed before her alarm went off just to express her concern about me. She had even used ordinary speech, rather than her high-flown Austenish. She heaped blame on herself—blame that belonged to me. I sternly resolved to take myself in hand. My period of pouting must cease. What were my feelings for a guy I had spoken to only one night, compared to the chief friendship of my entire life?

"I'm sorry I've been such a pill," I said. "Of course it's not you. Family things, and other stuff like that. I didn't mean to take it out on you."

Ashleigh looked at me keenly. "Other stuff like that, hmm? I think I know what's wrong. It's Ned, right? You're depressed because you can't see him. I know exactly how you feel. I wish I could see Parr too. E-mail helps, but it isn't enough. I wish we could be together in person! Under that dignity of his—that beautiful athletic bearing—he has such depths of kindness and strength, such good humor, such true manliness . . ." For a long time she continued in that vein, brushing twigs from her pajamas, as I forced myself to listen, and even to smile.

Chapter 10

Et tu, Samantha? ∾ *An Encounter with a Pirate* ∾
We prepare Speeches ∾ *Forefield again* ∾ *Disaster.*

And where was Samantha during my period of grief? Not around very much, especially after evening gymnastics practice got moved to Tuesdays, the time when I was most likely to see her. In my worst moments I considered hunting her down and laying my troubles at her feet, but in the end I always balked. My pain felt too raw.

So when she firmly straightened the drooping feather on my flapper hat as we were helping set up for our fathers' Halloween party and said, "Cheer up, Julie, I know how you feel, but it's not worth breaking your heart over," I almost dropped my bowl of gummi syringes.

Halloween may seem like a grisly theme for a pair of pediatricians to choose for their annual party, but it's very popular with their young patients. The greatest draw, I think, comes from the possibility that if they chose, Dad and Dr. Liu could spike the tomato juice with real blood.

"What's not worth what?" I stammered, thinking, Not Samantha too! Was everyone in my life hell-bent on interpreting my pain to suit their own needs?

"Cute blond princes up on a hill. Not worth crying over. The world's a big place—even Byzantium's a big place, comparatively—it's crawling with guys if you really want one. You don't need to get stuck on one particular unavailable guy. Unless you enjoy the melancholy, of course."

Sam is uncanny. It's as if she reads minds.

Ashleigh arrived before I could answer and dragged me off to help her arrange the jack-o'-lanterns to mimic the lighting effects of early-nineteenth-century candelabras. Then other guests arrived and kept her busy explaining that she was Jane Austen— Jane *Austen*, the writer—not a witch, a ghost, or Martha Washington.

Was Sam right? I wondered. Did I enjoy the melancholy? This was certainly a good time of year for it, with gusts of autumn wind blowing the storm clouds around and slapping the fallen leaves wetly against one's knees. I decided to take Sam's remarks to heart. When Ashleigh and I went to Emily Mehan's Halloween party the next night, I even tried flirting with Seth Young from my English class, the managing editor of *Sailing to B*. He was wearing a pirate costume, which made him look almost palatable. The red bandana he wore on his head gave his olive skin an appealing glow, and his blousy pirate shirt made him look lanky instead of skinny. An eye patch completed the romantic picture; I noticed for the first time that he had a nice nose. But his self-importance kept popping out from beneath the dangerous swagger he affected, and when he put his arm around me in the Mehans' backyard, I shrugged it off. Sam's advice might be good, but my heart just wasn't in it.

Ashleigh's mother came to pick us up before Seth could make any further moves, so I was spared having to reject him definitively and make future *Sailing* meetings awkward. At the lunchtime meeting the next day, he sat next to me but would not meet my eye. His face retained traces of pirate makeup, principally eyeliner, which I found obscurely embarrassing. When the fourth-period bell rang, I left quickly to avoid any possibility of conversation. He got up as if to follow, but evidently changed his mind when he saw Ashleigh waiting for me outside Ms. Nettleton's room.

"You've got to see this," she cried, grabbing my elbow and pulling me downstairs to the announcement board, which the Gerard twins were inspecting in postures of excitement (Yolanda, I assumed) and mild interest (Yvette).

"Look!" commanded Ashleigh with a sweeping gesture.

"What?" I asked. The twins' beaded heads blocked my view.

"Auditions," answered Ashleigh joyfully.

"Auditions?" Why would Ash care about auditions?

"At Forefield, for their musical," she elaborated.

"Forefield, get it?" said Yolanda. "The boys' school. That means not a lot of people auditioning for girls' parts. Wholly crisp—no Cordelia Nixon or Michelle Jeffries, 'cause they're in *West Side Story,* and who else from here is going to bother? I bet if we just show up, we can get parts, and if you can carry a tune, you can be a star. How about it, you want to be the heroine?" she asked her sister.

Yvette shook her head. "You can be the heroine. I'm playing the most important part," she said.

"What part's that?" said Yolanda. "They're not going to let you be the hero, silly, they have plenty of boys. And it says here, 'Directed by Benjamin Seward.' "

"No, silly, the audience."

I thought Yvette had the right idea. Acting in a play—a

musical, no less—was a frightening thought for someone as shy as me, not to mention the danger of a painful meeting with Parr. How much easier it would be, if Ash would only let me, to stay home and brood.

But *that*, I told myself, I must not do. No, seeing Parr and Ash together might be good for me, like cauterizing a wound to make it stop bleeding. In fact, I found myself almost hoping that I *would* see Parr: surely, a tempting little voice whispered, it would help me get over my troubles.

❧

The next problem Ash and I faced was finding suitable monologues for our auditions.

Ash naturally first thought of Darcy's proposal in *Pride and Prejudice*—the speech that begins, "In vain have I struggled. It will not do. My feelings will not be repressed. You must allow me to tell you how ardently I admire and love you."

Unfortunately, as we found when we consulted the book, that's also where the speech ends. Jane Austen tells us that "the avowal of all that he felt and had long felt for her immediately followed," but she doesn't specify what he says. The rest of the scene takes the form of a dialogue between the proud hero and offended heroine—deeply interesting to readers, but useless to auditioners.

We considered and rejected various alternatives, such as Mr. Collins's letter announcing his visit to the Bennet family and Lady Catherine de Bourgh's howl of disapproval at the thought that Elizabeth might become her niece by marrying Darcy. They were all either too brief or too deeply embedded in the novel's plot to stand alone.

"The problem is, it's a novel," I argued. "Don't you think we'd have better luck finding monologues if we looked at plays instead of books? Or movies, even."

"No drama could be more dramatic than the works of the great Miss Austen," said Ashleigh dismissively.

"Let's at least go down to the video store and see if we get any ideas," I urged.

She shot me the Mad Gleam. "My dear Julia, I believe you may have hit upon the solution! Perhaps some playwright or screenwriter may have supplied Miss Austen's missing words!" We rented three different *Pride and Prejudices*. After some discussion and much poking at the rewind button, Ash picked the Colin Firth version of Darcy's proposal and scribbled out a transcription.

For my audition piece, I chose Mercutio's Queen Mab speech in *Romeo and Juliet*. It's part of a scene in which Mercutio, my favorite character, mercilessly teases his cousin Romeo about being in love. He attributes Romeo's mooniness to a visit from Queen Mab, the fairy responsible for dreams. I chose it because I knew it practically by heart, having written a paper about it for the Nettle. Still, I tended to agree with Yolanda that the play was at least as silly as it was beautiful. The whole tragedy was so unnecessary! If Romeo and Juliet had just *talked* to each other, nobody would have had to die.

Besides being easy for me to memorize, the speech also had the advantage of being by Shakespeare, and therefore tough for a modern girl to deliver and even tougher for a modern listener to follow. Although I refused to let myself flub the audition on purpose, I secretly hoped that the difficulty of the material would keep me from getting a part. Then I'd be spared the pain of watching my best friend's budding relationship with my lost love.

⟋ᴏ

Mrs. Gerard drove Yolanda, Ashleigh, and me to Forefield for our auditions. As the car wound up the drive toward the school on the hill, I felt my insides quadrilling in a way that couldn't be explained by mere motion sickness.

"Break a leg, girls," said Mrs. Gerard, dropping us in front of the R. McNichol Robbins Theater Arts Center, behind the main classroom building. We pulled open the heavy bronze doors and followed signs into the theater, where a group of people clustered near the stage.

A spotlight reflected brightly off the hair of a slim, tallish figure, transforming my inner quadrille into a gymnastics meet. When he stepped aside, however, I saw that he was not the person I half hoped, half dreaded to see, but a brown-haired boy about the same height.

"Ashleigh! Julie!" called a male voice from the other side of the room. It set the trampolines going again briefly until I recognized it a split second later as Ned's bass. He bounded up the aisle to meet us. "You made it! Come meet Benjo and Ms. Wilson."

Ashleigh introduced Yolanda, and we followed Ned down to the front of the theater. Aside from one pale creature in a Sacred Heart uniform, we three were the only girls. "Hey, it's Erin from Sacred Heart," said Yolanda, running up to greet her. Chris Stevens—the boy who had shared my planter at the Columbus Cotillion—lounged beside Erin. He winked at me. Boys of various sizes punched each other and squirmed, or sat apart reviewing their monologues; some stared at us out of the corners of their eyes.

Benjo turned out to be the tallish, brown-haired guy who had so alarmed me. After a few minutes, during which a bell rang somewhere and additional aspiring actors arrived—including another Sacred Heart girl, this one quite young—he called for silence and addressed us. "Okay, let's get started. I'm Benjamin Seward, and I'll be directing *Midwinter Insomnia*, an original musical by Barry Davison, with music by Ned Downing and lyrics by Grandison Parr. That's Barry over there, and Ned's next to him, and Parr—where's Parr?—oh, I guess he's still at fencing practice. Anyway, most of you know Mr. Barnaby, our faculty adviser, and Ms. Wilson, our musical adviser." He indicated a bald, bearded man with a barrel chest and prominent ears and a slender, petite woman with straightened hair pulled back into a knot at her neck. Benjo continued, "When I call your name, please come up onstage and give your music to Tyler at the piano. All right? Alcott Fish."

A small boy presented himself, cleared his throat, sang "You're a Good Man, Charlie Brown" in a pretty soprano, recited a speech from the same play, and sat down again. The four directors whispered together, then called the next boy.

During the auditions that followed I had time to imagine various dire scenarios in which I fell off the stage, forgot my lines, changed key halfway through my song, fainted, laughed hysterically, or compulsively shouted *fire*; at last I decided to dull my thoughts by running through my speech over and over in my head.

When Erin's turn came, I stopped and paid close attention. By then Shakespeare's words in my head were beginning to sound dangerously like nonsense. She sang "My Favorite Things" with all the corn-syrup sweetness it deserves; her speech, from *The Glass Menagerie*, was similarly well articulated, sincere, and over-sweet.

Next came a striking boy with a dark complexion and a beautiful baritone. Then, after a few so-so singers and two pretty good younger boys, it was Yolanda's turn. Her rich alto, surprisingly sultry in someone so young, made a strong showing in "Too Darn Hot," from *Kiss Me, Kate*, and her speech from *Raisin in the Sun* moved me almost to tears.

Ashleigh, too, acquitted herself well, with a loud and tuneful rendition of "Take It Back" and a loud and passionate rendition of the Darcy proposal.

Then it was my turn. I made it onto the stage without falling over and handed my music to the boy at the piano. Things started out well enough, but I began to have second thoughts as I sang "It's All Right with Me." "It's the wrong time and the wrong place," the song begins (How true, how painfully true! I thought). But when I reached the part about trying to get over someone by throwing myself into someone else's arms, I felt Chris Stevens watching me slyly. By that time I wished I had chosen something else—anything else.

Still, despite my embarrassment, I managed to pronounce the words clearly and stay in tune. Relieved, I started in on my Queen Mab speech—but that too felt far more problematic on stage than it had in the safety of my attic bedroom. "She is the fairies' midwife, and she comes," said my mouth, while my mind, racing, chided me: What made you think it was a good idea to give a speech about fairies at a boys' school? How's that going to go over? I glanced cautiously around the audience—another bad idea. There was Ashleigh grinning at me, which had the perverse effect of making me more self-conscious; there was Chris Stevens, winking with his long cat's eyes; there was a little boy chewing the end of his pen and another sprawled out over two seats with his eyes closed, both radiating boredom; and there in the back—oh, horror! Had he been there the whole time?—stood Grandison Parr, tall and golden, looking right at me.

I panicked. My voice dropped to nothing. I rushed and mumbled my way to the end, stopping abruptly and cutting off the last three lines (which are kind of obscene anyhow). I dragged myself off the stage and sank into the dusty velvet seat beside Ashleigh's, where I wished I were dead.

The rest went by in an excruciating, slow-motion blur. Parr took the stage, and I sat, drinking in his pleasant, confident voice, with frozen limbs and cheeks that burned on and on through a thousand other speeches and meaningless songs. When the auditions were over, he came to find us. Ashleigh greeted him warmly, but I could hardly hear what she said over the pounding in my ears, nor could I choke out more than a monosyllable. All through the ride home, while Ashleigh and Yolanda eagerly reviewed the afternoon's events, I sat with my cheek pressed against the cool glass of the window, hardly blinking, hardly breathing. And the torture repeated itself all night long, first in my memory and then in my dreams, until I half hoped my blushes would set my sheets on fire, ending my misery in one magnificent blaze.

Chapter 11

Parts ∽ scripts ∽ rhymes ∽ songs ∽ an igsome Moth ∽
an Artistic Rivalry ∽ a direly misleading Scene involving a Sofa.

After the previous day's disaster, I walked the long way around to my first-period social studies class to avoid the bulletin board. I had no wish to see the cast list posted without my name. True, I had half hoped to tank at the audition; but half hoping to tank is one thing, actually tanking quite another.

In the end, my careful detour came to nothing. Ashleigh and Yolanda appeared at my lunch table waving a piece of paper.

"Good afternoon, Headmistress Lytle," cried the Enthusiast.

I frowned impatiently. I was in no mood for Ashleigh's play-acting. "What are you talking about?" I said.

"Look!" said Yolanda. She put the page down in front of me, just missing a pool of spilled mustard. "It's your part—you got a 'little' part—Headmistress Lytle—see? And there's me, I'm Tanya, president of the student body—I hope I get lots of lines—and Ashleigh's Hermia, and that's it from Byz High. We figured it was okay to take the poster down, since nobody else from here tried out. But Erin got a part too—she's Helen. And Emma Caballero, that freshman from Sacred Heart, she's Chloe."

"Is this not good news?" said Ashleigh. "Grandison Parr plays Owen, captain of the debate team, and your beloved Ned is the musical director, so you will have frequent opportunities to converse with him during rehearsals."

"Oh, are you going out with that guy Ned?" said Yolanda. "Crisp! You never told me that. He seems like a really nice guy. I kind of liked that tall guy with the nice voice—he was cute. I wonder if he got a part. He had to, he had the best voice there. Which one do you think he is? Kevin Rodriguez? Ravi Rajan? Ask your boyfriend, okay? Oh, but don't tell Adam!" Adam White, a junior, was sometimes the man in Yolanda's life.

"Ned's not my boyfriend," I protested. "I only met him twice."

"Yes, but you called him a Darcy, remember? Pay her no mind, Yolanda, she is too modest to admit her true feelings," said Ashleigh.

"Whatever," I said testily. The alternating waves of anticipation and terror, disappointment and relief, which had been sweeping over me for the past few weeks, had taken their toll on my usually even temper.

But how had I gotten a part, after such a spectacularly bad performance at the audition? Ash and Yolanda insisted that I had sung sweetly and spoken well, though softly at the end. But I knew they were just trying to make me feel better. No, the only possible explanation was lucky (or unlucky) chance. Five girls had auditioned—five had been cast. If a sixth had shown up at the tryouts, she would surely have won the part of Headmistress Lytle.

❧

Nicole Rossi, Ashleigh's mother, picked up our scripts for us at Forefield that evening on her way home from work.

While *Midwinter Insomnia* may not be the very silliest play I've ever read, it's up there. It takes place in a boarding school rather like Forefield, but coed. The scene opens with romantic mixups among the fifth formers, or juniors: Xander (played by Ravi Rajan) is going out with Hermia (Ashleigh); Daniel (Chris Stevens, apparently typecast) is trying to steal her away; and Helen (Erin) has a hopeless crush on Daniel. Meanwhile, Owen, the captain of the debate team (Parr), and Tanya, the president of the student body (Yolanda), are having a lovers' quarrel over a third former (that is, a freshman), formerly a member of the debate club, whom Tanya has enticed to serve on the student council, which meets at the same time, therefore forcing him to quit debate. To punish her, Owen convinces his younger brother, Rob (Alcott Fish), a science geek, to sneak into the chem lab and create a love potion that he can give Tanya, causing her to fall for the ridiculous Butthead (Kevin Rodriguez), who plays Romeo in the middle school's laughable production of *Romeo and Juliet*. When Rob mischievously taints a drinking fountain with the love potion, Xander, Hermia, Daniel, and Helen begin a game of musical partners that ends only with the grand finale.

I played the headmistress, Miss Lytle, who puts in occasional appearances calling for order, scolding mischief makers, and presiding over the happy ending. She also sings a duet with the dean of students, a cameo appearance by Forefield's actual dean, Mr. Hanson. Altogether, she has eleven lines, not counting the duet.

I was afraid they would be eleven lines too many.

"I envy Yolanda—oh! how I envy her," said Ashleigh, squeezing Juniper until he gave a reproachful kitten squeak.

"She does have more songs, but you have more lines," I pointed out.

"Faugh! Little do I care for lines and songs! It's the *kisses* that I envy. She gets to kiss Grandison Parr!"

"Yes, but you get to kiss Ravi Rajan—isn't that the guy Yolanda thinks is so cute? Maybe you'll be so swept away, you'll forget all about Parr."

Ashleigh gave me her look of Reproach Tinged with Disgust. "Forget! Forget Grandison Parr! Ask me to forget my own name—my father and mother—my native tongue—the points of the compass—I will forget what it means to be human before I forget Grandison Parr!"

⁓

As for me (I thought with a sigh), I had better forget Grandison Parr before I forgot what it meant to be human. In the weeks that followed, I came much closer to that goal.

Not that I ever managed true forgetfulness: how could I, when I saw him at least twice a week at rehearsals? But practice made my heart grow tougher, like a blister that breaks and hardens to a callus, until I could smile at him, answer his remarks in sentences longer than a word or two, and even meet his eyes.

The hardest moment was my first rehearsal, when I felt him watching me. It took all my willpower to obey Benjo and focus on my character's quarrel with the dean—far too lenient a man, in Miss Lytle's opinion. When Benjo directed me to stamp my foot, turn my back on the dean, and face the audience, I trained my eyes on the exit sign until I could bear to look at them directly. After a week or two, though, I grew used to having an audience.

Talking to Parr took even more courage, but I found I couldn't avoid it. Although Ashleigh and I had relatively few scenes with him, he made a point of seeking out our company.

"Hey," he said, coming up behind me as I was helping Ashleigh go over her lines before the second rehearsal, "can either of you think of a better rhyme for Hermia? Barry says *germier* is revolting, and anyway, I'm not even sure it's a word."

"*Wormier?*" suggested Ashleigh.

"*Wormier?* Hmm, I hadn't thought of that. It's . . . a possibility," said Parr.

"Oh, Ash, ig! That's even more revolting," I said.

"All right, *squirmier? Sp*—no—well, *you* think of something then, Julie, I have the highest confidence in your abilities. Julie writes poetry, you know," she told Parr.

He turned to me keenly. "Do you?"

"Oh, Ash," I moaned, feeling squirmier myself. "Not much, and it's not any good."

"What do you mean, it's not good?" cried the loyal Enthusiast. "What about that beautiful poem you wrote in seventh grade about the sunset and—"

I moved quickly to stop her, before she could recite one of my juvenile efforts; she likes my older, flowerier poems the best. "I know!" I said. "What about *hypothermia?*"

"Brilliant! That's perfect, Julia, thank you!" said Parr, making a motion as if to hug me. Startled, I drew back, and his gesture trailed off into awkwardness; but he continued to grin at me. He had very white teeth. I loved the way he called me by the formal version of my name—it made me feel like a grander version of myself.

"See, I told you she'd think of something," said Ashleigh proudly. "You can always count on Julie."

Although these moments with Parr were the shaky high points of my days, I naturally spent more time with Ned, who ran the musical rehearsals and stood in as my singing partner, the dean, for Dean Hanson, who rarely made it to rehearsals. The more I saw of Ned, the more I liked him. His tunes were so catchy that I often found myself singing them around the house, and more than once I noticed my mother humming "Who Would Want to Hook Up with Helen?" or "Oh Lord, What Fools!" And I soon came to appreciate Ned's good nature as well as his music. In a room full of big egos—Benjo, Barry, Chris, Erin in her quiet way, Ravi—Ned's was a hardworking and self-forgetful presence. He reminded me of another friend, a person of boundless energy and loyal encouragement: Ashleigh. Most musical directors would have lost their patience long ago, I was sure. Ned, though, never stopped encouraging me.

"That's great, Julie," he said. "You got a much bigger sound that time. Remember how quiet you were last week? Okay, now this time focus on the deer head across the room. You want to really make his ears curl. Great! That was great, now this time let's see if you can really concentrate on keeping from going flat on the high notes. Nice and loud! Yes! Yes! Listen to you! Okay, I think maybe I pushed you too far that time, you went a little sharp. Not 'ah,' more like 'ah.' Try it again. Good! Ashleigh, did you hear that? Did you hear how great Julie's sounding? That was really good, Julie, and you were definitely loud enough if Ashleigh heard you all the way over by the door."

At first I was so caught up in learning my lines, governing my heart, and training my voice not to slink off with its tail between my tonsils that I had no time to watch my fellow actors. But as I grew more accustomed to the scene around me (except for Parr kissing Yolanda—I never grew accustomed to that), I began to notice several dramas.

The most obvious, because it touched me personally, involved Chris Stevens. Chris tried to ooze his way into the good graces of every girl in the production, with the sole exception of Emma Caballero, who was too young even for him. He persisted like an elegant insect, gently dodging any slaps and returning to buzz and brush against you. His technique involved floating around nearby and implying that *you* were interested in *him*.

"Sorry I didn't see you much last time, Julie," he said soon after we started rehearsals. "I was in the trophy room with Erin and couldn't get away. But I don't want you to feel I was neglecting you."

"Don't worry, Chris, I don't," I told him. "Actually, I'd prefer it if you *did* neglect me."

As I soon learned, this was the wrong approach to take with Chris, who took resistance as a challenge. Far from keeping him away, it drew him to me as pheromones might draw a monstrous moth. I had learned all about pheromones during Ashleigh's insect craze. Chris fluttered softly near me, fanning his vast, pale wings and reaching out with his hairy feelers. Ig!

Yolanda's approach—treating his advances with friendly, offhand patience—worked far better. "Chris, how'd you get back there? Sorry, I keep stepping on you! Did I hurt your toe? Hey, didn't you call me last night? Sorry, I meant to call you back—I didn't forget about you, I swear, it's just that I had a lot of homework, and then I was talking to Ravi, and then it got late, and anyway, don't they make you turn off your phones after ten?" Something about her careless solicitude kept him, if not at arm's length, at least at elbow's.

Oblivious Ashleigh didn't respond to his attentions at all, since she didn't notice them. But Erin, poor thing, responded all too well. She developed an obvious, violent crush on him. Chris tormented her by ignoring her most of the time, giving her just enough attention to keep her going, and flirting with the rest of us whenever he saw her watching.

"Where's Chris?" asked Erin one afternoon after we'd been rehearsing for several weeks. "We're supposed to go over the scene where I give him the answers to the math test."

"I last saw him with Yolanda," said Ashleigh. "He said something about showing her the trophy room."

Erin stiffened. "I'd better go find him," she said, and she hurried off.

Kevin Rodriguez and little Alcott Fish giggled.

"What's so amusing?" asked Ashleigh.

Alcott turned pink.

"You know, the trophy room? With all the sofas and everything?" said Kevin.

"What about it?"

Alcott turned pinker, and Kevin rolled his eyes.

"Oh, grow up, guys," said Ravi. "It's supposed to be where people go to—where people go for privacy," he explained.

～

Of the actors, the most talented by far were Ravi, Alcott, and Kevin, who turned out to be a surprise comic genius. As Butthead, the boorish boy playing Romeo in the play within a play, he overacted with such flawless control that he never once overdid overdoing it. When Yolanda's Tanya drank Rob's love potion and fell for Butthead, Kevin turned into a parody of Chris Stevens subtle enough that Chris himself never noticed, yet broad enough to keep the rest of us choking back laughter. Yolanda deepened the impression by putting a touch of lovesick Erin into her Tanya, but only a touch. Either she didn't want to be cruel to her old friend, or she was acting unconsciously, not quite aware of her influences.

Ravi was a delight to watch and listen to: handsome, lithe, with a voice like honey and butter. I could see why Yolanda had a thing for him. Ash, I thought, was lucky to have her heart already occupied, or after their first kiss in rehearsals she would have been as bad as Erin with Chris. But although Ravi clearly knew the impression he made, there was nothing wolfish or manipulative about him. He accepted admiration as his due and repaid it with friendly attention, as if to suggest that a warm admiration for Ravi was a pleasure that you and he could share.

Tensions ran high between Benjo, the director, and Barry, the playwright, who attended every rehearsal and held strong opinions about how we should deliver his beloved lines. Young Emma—as Chloe, the middle schooler playing Juliet in the laughable play-within-a-play—had an uncontrollable tendency to giggle. Unable to curb this habit, Benjo used it as a way of showing up the silliness of the middle schoolers' production. But Barry couldn't stand it. He snapped, "Stop giggling!" at poor Emma whenever she so much as smiled, which made her giggle even more.

"I can't—I can't—I c—I can't help—!" gurgled poor Emma.

"Barry, quit messing up my actors! I mean it! You're making her choke," said Benjo.

"Your so-called actors are messing up my play. Can't you control them?" said Barry, stepping closer.

"What needs controlling is *you* need to control *yourself*. Leave now, please!"

"Leave? Leave this mess with *you*?"

Both guys, I saw, had clenched their jaws and fists. Any minute they would come to blows. Fortunately, Parr saw it too and stepped in. "Hey, Barry, do you have a sec? I rewrote the chorus to 'Queen of the Ice,' and I want to know what you think."

Benjo was still glaring at Barry, so I decided to distract him too. "Benjo, can I ask you a quick question? Should I exit while the dean is still singing, or should I wait till he's done?" Benjo seemed annoyed at the interruption, but Parr repaid me with a grateful look.

Because my part was so small, I had plenty of time to observe all these offstage dramas. When not rehearsing my scenes, I made myself useful as a page turner, prop fetcher, and prompter. I learned Yolanda's part before she did herself.

Was I foolish to watch her scenes with Parr, exposing myself over and over to their kisses? Perhaps, but I couldn't keep away, and they seemed to find my presence useful.

～○

One day while I was helping Ned go over the drinking-fountain song with Alcott and Kevin, Alcott threw his beaker full of love potion at the fountain with a little too much zest. It shattered.

He leaped back. "Hey, wasn't that supposed to be safety glass?"

"Good thing it broke now, not during a performance," said Ned. "We need to find something stronger. Plastic or metal."

"Like a loving cup, maybe," I joked. "The trophy room's full of them."

"A loving cup for the love potion—ha! Julie, that's brilliant. Wait there, I'll be right back." Ned ran off.

Parr, who was nearby helping Benjo choreograph the big fight scene between Daniel and Xander, saw him go. "Oh, no, Ned, don't do that! Quick, somebody, stop him," he said.

"Stop what? Where's he going?" asked Alcott.

"The trophy room, obviously. If Wattles catches him taking a trophy, that's it for his scholarship."

"I got it," I volunteered, feeling responsible.

I thought I remembered the way to the trophy room, from my bathroom adventures at the Columbus Cotillion. However, it took me longer than I expected to find it. By the time I got there, Ned was perched on tiptoe on the back of a green leather sofa, trying to pry open a trophy-case door with a protractor.

Something was clearly about to snap. I hoped it would be the protractor, but the door looked more likely.

"Ned! Stop!"

"Oh, hi, Julie—give me a hand up here, will you? I've almost got it."

"Stop it, Ned, you're going to break the case!"

"No, I'm not, I've almost got it—"

As he levered the protractor, the case begin to tilt. I scrambled up on the sofa to pull him away before everything fell. Our joint weight made the sofa tip, and we both lost our footing on the slippery leather, landing in a tangle on the seat. Fortunately, the trophy case stayed where it was.

"Julie, are you okay?"

"Ouch!"

"Sorry, was that your leg? Why'd you do that, anyway? I almost had it!"

He tried to get up, but I grabbed him around the neck and shoulders and hung on tight. "Stop, Ned! Think of your scholarship."

"But it would be so perfect," he said, squirming.

Just then the door opened and Ashleigh and Erin burst in.

"Oh! Jul—Ned—forgive me, I didn't mean to intrude," said Ashleigh, backing out and pulling Erin with her.

"Ash, wait!" I yelled, but by the time I had untangled myself from Ned and talked him into leaving the loving cups in their cases, she was long gone.

◡๏

The scene in the trophy room dashed my hopes of convincing Ashleigh that my feelings toward Ned were nothing more than friendship. "I was just trying to stop him from stealing a loving cup to use as a prop," I protested, but it was no use. Even I could hear how lame it sounded. "You can ask Parr, he told me to go," I added feebly.

"Did he? Did he indeed aid Ned in planning an assignation? Clearly *Parr's* friend confides in *him* far more trustingly than *mine* does in *me*," said Ashleigh, working up to full-blown Austenese. "No, no! Say no more! Far be it from me to pry from you a confidence that you do not willingly surrender! But if it were me, you know *I'd* tell *you*."

"Ash, I swear, there's nothing to tell."

"Because we interrupted you."

"No, because we weren't doing anything. But what were *you* doing there, anyway?"

"Erin was looking for Chris, and Kevin said you'd gone to the trophy room. I thought you might need protecting. Little did I imagine what scenes we would interrupt! Next time, tell me and I'll guard the door for you."

Chapter 12

I keep up my grades ∾ My father grouses ∾
A Turkey again ∾ Rehearsals.

Have you ever noticed how once teachers get an idea into their heads, it's easier to interrupt a bus of kids singing "100 Bottles of Beer on the Wall" than to change their minds? This is why, if you have limited time for study, it's best to apply it at the beginning of the semester. If you do, most teachers will dismiss you early on as a good student and not look too hard for mistakes.

What with *Insomnia* and *Sailing to B.*, my hours available for homework plummeted. My grades, however, rose. My B-pluses puffed up to A-minuses, my A-minuses to full-out A's. One would think such a state of affairs would please my father. But no: he considered two time-consuming extracurriculars one too many. "You want to appear well rounded, not dilettantish," he said. "If you had more time to study, you could push those minus marks up to straight A's."

Dropping *Sailing* was tempting, but it seemed unwise. By putting me in the good graces of the Nettle, my work on the magazine probably saved me hours that I would otherwise have had to spend preparing for class by second-guessing her opinions. And although I half longed to give up *Insomnia*, I felt I couldn't let down the other actors. I explained to Dad that I had plenty of time, really, now that the fall foliage-viewing rush was over at Helen's Treasures.

Amy rolled her eyes slightly at the mention of my mother's business, but she took my side. "Julie's learning follow-through, Steve. Colleges value that," she told my father. She even volunteered to drive me to and from rehearsals when they met on Tuesdays.

One Tuesday, then, in the middle of November, she dropped me off half an hour early on her way to meet a client. It was unseasonably warm. I unbuttoned my coat and sat on the steps of the Robbins Center to wait for Benjo or Mr. Barnaby, who both had keys.

The first person to arrive at the center that afternoon, however, was not the director or faculty adviser, but Turkeyface from the Columbus Cotillion. When he saw me, his face turned red— or rather, redder.

"What are you doing here, young woman?" he spat. "Don't you know this is a boys' school?"

"I'm just waiting for Benjo Seward," I said. "He's—"

He cut me off. "Don't go trying to implicate Benjamin Seward. He would never sneak a girl onto campus. He's a responsible young man. He knows the rules."

As Turkeyface lectured me, Grandison Parr appeared over his shoulder. "Hello, Julia," he said.

Turkeyface spun around. "I knew it!" he gloated. "Not only is your girlfriend here on campus illegally, but she was trying to blame Seward!"

"But Julia's—" began Parr.

"Not a word! One word buys you three demerits. You're both coming with me to see the dean."

He took us each by a shoulder and marched us to the administration building.

Dean Hanson's door was ajar. "What's up, Matthew?" asked the dean, looking up from his computer. "Oh, hello, Julie—Grandison. What can I do for you? I *have* been practicing—I promise—listen:

If you force me to be harsh, I'll
Try my best to be impartial,
But a carrot's always better than the most effective stick.

I sang back the next verse:

My dear dean, you're much too soft—when
I remember just how often
Your supposed angels misbehave, I swear, it makes me sick!

"Cool beans, Julie! Sounding good!" said the dean.

"You know this girl?" sputtered Turkeyface.

"Of course I do—she's Headmistress Lytle."

"Headmistress? *Headmistress?*"

"Yes, and an excellent one too. Way better than my dean. Of course, she rehearses way more. You look puzzled, Matthew. *Midwinter Insomnia.* The musical, man, the musical! What's up—is there a problem?"

"Well! No, not if you know this girl. I expect you know your own business. Forgive me. I would never interfere." Turkeyface made his exit.

The three of us waited until the door clicked shut before laughing. "Matthew obviously agrees with Miss Lytle that I'm much too soft," said Dean Hanson. "But actually, you're the ones who are too soft on *me*. Barnaby's right, I should make it to more rehearsals. Come on, let's get down to the theater."

"Are girls really not allowed on campus?" I asked as we walked back along the gravel to the Robbins Center.

"No way—did Matthew tell you that? I guess, technically, nonstudents aren't allowed except under special circumstances— which covers things like playing the headmistress in the school play, so you're okay there. And, of course, girls tend to be non-students at a boys' school. But there's nothing in the charter for-bidding girls per se. Matthew gets a little carried away with rules. He's a—well, a—hmm . . ." Dean Hanson trailed off, evidently remembering his position as a member of the administration speaking about a member of the faculty to students (or, in this case, a student and a nonstudent). He collected himself and began again: "So, Grandison, what do you think of the Saberteeth's chances against Groton this season?"

"I'm a little worried, actually. The Teeth are facing some se-rious competition. Groton's got Dashwood now, so of course that gives them an edge over last year. I can't really blame him for transferring—coed's a temptation," said Parr, glancing at me. "But I wish he'd waited another year. Bloom and Coe are going to be killer once they get their footing, but they're not there yet."

The Saberteeth's prospects took us the rest of the way to the Robbins Center, where the cast was waiting for us somewhat impatiently. Ned was delighted to see the dean, whose presence kept me busy, for once; the two of us worked hard on our duet all through the rehearsal. "Nice, Julie—you're sounding very dis-approving," said Ned. "You could even pump up the resentment, if you want. Go ahead and squeak on that high G. Mr. Hanson, you're doing well with the sheepish expression, but if you could find the time to rehearse more, you might remember more of the lyrics."

Some of the others came over to watch the dean and me while they waited for Ned to listen to their songs. "Oh, well done, well done, my dearest Julia," cried Ashleigh. "And you too, Dean— well done! Julia, you are indeed fortunate that the dean himself, at heart, shares those qualities which make his character so infuriating to the headmistress. It must greatly ease your task of acting stern. For my part, I find it difficult to maintain the necessary anger at Xander's coldness, since Ravi himself is the soul of kindliness."

"That's nice of you to say, but ouch!" said Ravi. "You certainly slapped me like somebody angry."

"That's just Ashleigh's natural enthusiasm," said Ned. "She gets carried away."

"It was my duty as an actress—it was the least I could do," said Ash. "If it's any comfort to you, I slapped Chris harder. Speaking of which, some charitable soul ought to go rescue Yolanda. I saw Chris follow her into the lighting booth."

"Not me," I said. "You'd just have to send someone else to rescue me next."

"I'll go," said Parr quickly. "Yolanda and I should be practicing anyway."

❧

Amy's meeting ran late, making me the last of the girls left at Forefield after rehearsal. Parr and Ned sat with me on the Robbins Center steps to wait for her. The dregs of pink drained from the sky and a cold wind started up; Parr moved down a step to put his body between me and the wind.

"Why are you at Forefield if you'd rather go to a coed school?" I asked him.

"It's a family tradition. My father and his father and his father and *his* father and the rest of their fathers went to Forefield, back to when it was just five pupils and a scandalous headmaster. Did you know the first head got thrown out of England for killing a horse in a duel? The man he was fighting survived, but the horse died. Apparently it was a very important horse."

"Parr's great-great-great-great-grandpa, I mean great-great-great-great-grand-Parr, is one of the boys in the frieze carved over the fireplace in the Great Hall. He's the one on the far left, with the funny ears. Hard to get a hat over them," said Ned.

"Hey, Noodles, quit putting hats on my ancestors—I mean it," said Parr, cuffing Ned gently.

"I never put a hat on your ancestor," said Ned. "Like I just said, his ears stick out too much."

"Anyway, though, Dad would be heartbroken if I didn't go to Forefield," continued Parr. "We don't exactly see eye to eye on everything, so I assume I'm going to be disappointing him enough later on—I might as well let him win what he can now, before the real battle starts." He paused, then added, "The boy-girl ratio isn't so bad at Forefield this year, though, with the play."

"What about you, Ned—do you mind the all-boys thing?" I asked.

"Oh, well, I wouldn't say I *like* it, but I can't really complain. They're giving me a scholarship. Apparently Grandison's great-great-grandpa—or somebody's great-great-grandpa, anyway—

thought the gramophone was destroying society by letting people play records instead of musical instruments. He endowed a
scholarship for musicians. The only catch is that I'm not allowed
to make any records while I'm at Forefield, or even listen
to them."

"No records?" I exclaimed. "Does that mean no CDs? How
can you stand it?"

"Fortunately, the trustees interpret that to mean ancient stuff
like wax tubes and 78s—the kind of records that were around
when the scholarship was started. They said it's fine for me to
listen to anything digital."

"That wasn't my ancestor," said Parr. "Can you imagine anyone related to my father endowing a scholarship for music? Tin-
ear Charlie himself? Although it would be almost like my
grandfather to make sure a musician wasn't allowed to listen to
music. He has strong ideas about what's worth spending time on.
My father too, but he's not as mean about it."

"My father's kind of like that too," I said. "He's always bug-
ging me to do more extracurriculars so I can get into college,
and then telling me that my extracurriculars are bringing my
grades down."

"Is he why you tried out for *Insomnia*?" asked Parr.

"Yes—sort of, pretty much," I said.

"Thank God for our fathers, then," said Parr. "Otherwise—"

Amy drove up just then and honked, so I didn't get to hear
why Parr was grateful for our fathers. He opened the car door for
me, extracting a sour smile of approval from Amy, who sets great
store by courtesy. As we drove off, I wondered what he had been
about to say.

Chapter 13

My mother gives up ~ Thanksgiving ~ yet another Turkey ~ an Identity Crisis ~ a Comeuppance.

*W*hen I got home from school the next day, my mother was packing away the Halloween merchandise and bringing out the Christmas things.

"Don't we usually do that after Thanksgiving?" I said.

Mom finished unwrapping a tin Santa and sat back on her heels. She looked up at me seriously. "Hi, honey. I thought we'd better try to catch whatever traffic there is from the Thanksgiving weekenders while we still can. I didn't get that job I was hoping for, so I'm going to work for the Nick-Nack Barn. They may not pay much, but it's steady and I get health insurance. They want me to start right after Thanksgiving."

"Oh, God, Mom, I'm sorry," I said. The Nick-Nack Barn, a heartless, tasteless chain two towns south, was my mother's ugliest rival.

"I'm not," said my mother. "Don't look so gloomy. It's just until I find something better. It won't be so bad—the manager's a nice woman, she's letting me do the window displays, and I can open Helen's Treasures on weekends. Want to give me a hand with these things?"

"Sure," I said. "I just have to send some e-mail first. I promised

Eleanor—she's our editor at *Sailing*—that I'd let her and Seth know what I think about a couple of poems we're considering."

⌒

Mom and I didn't have long to set up and sell the Christmas stock before Thanksgiving was upon us.

I won't dwell on this bitter holiday, which I spent with my stepmother and her family. I would naturally have preferred my mother's company, but I wasn't given a choice: it was Dad and Amy's turn to have me. I biked over, envying the wild turkeys that vanished into the trees in a pale whir of feathers as I passed. If they had been shot, plucked, roasted with rosemary and lemons, and set on the table to be torn to pieces by Amy's critical mother, her prune-faced brother, his cowed wife, and their four boisterous, self-satisfied little boys, would the turkeys have had a worse time than I had?

I will admit that the food was good. Of course it was: Amy made it. No soggy Brussels sprouts and cardboard stuffing for her. We had vegetables that snapped gently when you bit them, squash roasted to melting depth, fresh citrus-cranberry sauce, and turkey whose tenderness remained uncompromised by the crispness of its skin.

"Amy, when are you and Steve going to give me a grand-daughter?" asked my stepgrandmother, helping herself to the last slice of white meat. "It looks like I'm getting nothing but boys out of Mark and Susie."

Amy went pale. Taking pity on her, I spilled some lemon-rosemary gravy on her mother's blouse.

The distraction worked. Beneath Amy's scolding, I detected a wisp of gratitude. But my act of generosity put me in disgrace with the family for the rest of the weekend, so I was doubly glad to get home that Sunday, especially after a weekend in my new, dark basement room.

I found my mother on Ashleigh's roof with my friend and her father, helping install their annual Christmas display. This invariably involved Santa and his sleigh, but the Rossis relied on my mother to give each year's display a distinctive character. During Ashleigh's King Arthur phase, for example, Mom had made Santa into a knight and the reindeer into unicorns. Last year she had made Santa fly over the Manhattan skyline, which she outlined in Christmas lights. When I arrived, Joe Rossi was urging Mom to make the reindeer's antlers into menorahs, in honor of our family's heritage. She thanked him, but declined.

This year Santa was much slenderer than usual. He was wearing a top hat and a tall collar.

"Looks crisp!" I called up to them.

"Oh, honey, you're back! You look so short down there," my mother called down.

"The door's open—come on up," shouted Joe.

"No, that's okay, I'm done up here," said Mom. "Hang on, I'll be right down. Oh, Ashleigh, are you coming too?" The two of them vanished through the roof's trapdoor (I could have told her, but didn't, that the tree made a quicker and easier route), and emerged at the front door. Joe waved at us from the roof, where he stayed to admire their handiwork.

"How do you like Mr. Darcy as Santa?" said Ash as the three of us went into Helen's Treasures. "Ned suggested putting bonnets on the reindeer, but when your mother tried it, they wouldn't go over the antlers."

"Oh, that's Darcy? Do you think playing Santa is really in character for him? Seems more like something Mr. Bingley would do," I said.

"Very well, Mr. Bingley, if you prefer," said Ash. "Most people seem to think it's someone from *A Christmas Carol*, anyway. Philistines! So how was your Thanksgiving? Were your step-cousins there? Was it utterly unsupportable?"

"Yes, did you have a nice time, honey? Aunt Ruth sends her love," said Mom. "She gave me a new coat that Molly's grown out of already. It should fit you. That girl's growing even faster than you are. Oh! and one of your friends came by the shop on Wednesday and left something for you. Wait a sec, I think I put it in the desk." She rummaged around for a while and came out with a small package.

"Who was it?" I said. "One of the Gerard twins?"

"No, a boy. Nice-looking young man. He introduced himself, but I'm sorry to say I was a little distracted and I don't remember his name. It was busy here Wednesday. I sold all the reindeer soap."

"What did he look like?" said Ashleigh. "Was he of middle stature, about Julia's height, with lightish brown hair and deep, soulful brown eyes?"

"Um, he could have been. I'm sorry—I should have noticed better. I forgot you girls are getting to the age when you need all the details you can get about boys."

Casting reproachful glances at Mom, Ashleigh and I carried the package upstairs to my attic.

"It's from Ned, I know it is! Does it have a note? Open it!" cried Ash, bouncing wildly.

"No note, but there's writing on the box." I read: "*Had*

enough wattles this season? If not, here's sweets for the sweet. Yours ever— I can't read the name."

"Let's see! That must be *E*-something-*D*—what's Ned's middle name?"

"Does he even have one? That looks nothing like an *E*. More like a *C*. Chris Stevens? Could that be possible? Too bad it's so smudged," I said.

"Of course it's an *E*—well, I guess it could be an *N*—*N*, *E*, *D*, maybe?"

"How do you get an *N* from that? It's got to be a *C* or a *G*, or maybe a sloppy script *A*—something open on the right—well, I guess it *could* be a really messy capital *E*, but for sure it's no *N*. Here, give it back, let's see what's inside."

The box contained a gorgeous chocolate turkey, its plumage delicately marked in three colors of chocolate: dark, milk, and white.

"Sweets for the sweet! Is that not a chivalrous thought? That settles it—it must be from Ned."

"Or whoever sent it could be calling me a turkey," I said.

"Nonsense, Ned would never suggest such a thing. He has too kind a heart."

"Why would Ned give me a chocolate turkey?"

"Oh, Julia! Do not pretend you do not know! Chivalrous young men courted their chosen ladies with gifts of sweetmeats even in King Arthur's time. As for the turkey—well, it *is* Thanksgiving."

Whatever Ashleigh said, I didn't believe Ned was the turkey giver. For one thing, he couldn't spell—or at least, he couldn't type. Of course, the note was handwritten; that could explain the absence of typos. Still, it didn't sound like his style. But if not

Ned, who? Chris Stevens, Mr. Igsome himself? Unappetizing thought! Seth Young? Dean Hanson, perhaps, as an apology for his turkey-faced colleague's treatment? Surely not: my mother would never call the dean a boy; and similar reasoning ruled out Zach Liu, since she would have recognized him. Grandison Parr, then? Possibly. The reference to wattles suggested, if not the dean, then Ned or Parr. Nibbling on a bit of the tail—first-rate chocolate—I felt my heart begin to beat faster. From the sugar? Or from a powerful feeling that I would not allow myself to put into words?

But would my unspoken hopes turn out to be hollow after all—as hollow as the chocolate turkey that was vanishing before my eyes?

And whoever the kind turkey giver was, how would I express my gratitude? Obviously, I couldn't just thank all the candidates, or the ones who hadn't given me any chocolate would think I had left my mental marshmallows in the microwave a bit too long.

After some deliberation, I sent e-mail to Ned, Parr, and Seth, thanking them in general terms for their recent kindness, and slipping in a reference to Thanksgiving. I hoped that the innocent guys—the ones who hadn't sent me a turkey—would conclude that the theme of the holiday had made me think grateful thoughts. As for the chocolate giver, I hoped he would interpret my message as a response to his gift.

And if the turkey had come from Chris, he could just consider me rude. He would get no thanks from me. I hadn't asked him to shower me with turkeys. He would have to do more than ply me with chocolate to worm his way into my good graces.

I received the following answers.

From Parr:
Dear Julia, What a sweet message. But it's the other way around—
I'm the lucky one. CGP.

From Ned:
happy thangsgiving to you too julie. i am glad you and ashleigh are
in the play its much more fun than any ohter year!

From Seth:
Hi, Julie. I was touched to receive your message. I hope you
enjoyed your Thanksgiving, and I look forward to seeing you when
school resumes. Yours, Seth.

Inconclusive, I thought. Nobody either acknowledged or repudiated the turkey. Well, at least if it was one of them, he wouldn't think me rude and ungrateful.

༝

After the holiday, the pace picked up at school. Final papers and exams approached, and the deadline loomed for the winter issue of *Sailing*. Work on *Midwinter Insomnia* slowed dramatically, however, since finals were an even bigger deal at Forefield than at Byzantium High. With rehearsal time given over to review sessions, our schedule shrank to a weekly rehearsal, "the minimum we can meet and still expect to have anything left to forget by the time we get to winter break," as Benjo put it.

My part was so small, and my partner, the dean, so rarely around during these weeks, that I had almost nothing to do but prompt the others. I spent my time watching Ashleigh (as Hermia) chase after Ravi (as Xander) and defend herself from Igsome Chris's accusations of coldness.

As Daniel, Chris sang:

Half an hour of hanging out with Hermia
Would give a seal or walrus hypothermia.
She's the Queen of the Ice.
She doesn't know the meaning of nice.
Turn the thermostat up and crank it!
I need another sweater and a blanket.

Ash/Hermia responded,

Insinuating snake!
He's a man on the make,
Out to get what he can take,
And take what he can get—
Which is nothing . . . yet.

The *yet* came as Hermia drank the tainted water and found herself falling under his spell.

Whenever Chris saw me watching him in his scenes with Ashleigh, he would give me a horrible, languid smile.

I naturally took frequent breaks from their rehearsals to torture myself by watching Parr and Yolanda quarrel passionately, then kiss and make up.

One day shortly before winter break, when Ashleigh's dad drove us to Forefield, I noticed that Yolanda was uncharacteristically quiet. She contributed almost nothing to our discussion of the dance number leading up to the grand finale (which I found too energetic, whereas Ashleigh considered it not energetic enough).

"You okay, Landa?" I asked.

"Fine."

"It's just, you seem subdued."

"Subdued? Oh, I—sorry, I was thinking about something else. What were you saying?"

"The finale. Too tame? Too wild?"

"I like it the way it is. It's, uh, kind of energetic but not all that energetic, if you see what I'm saying. And that's what it should be like, because it's the finale."

Although Yolanda does not always think through what she's going to say before she says it, this remark seemed especially incoherent. It made me wonder.

Arriving at Forefield, however, I turned my attention to my part and forgot about the conversation until much later in the afternoon, when I went to help Yolanda and Parr. They were rehearsing alone in the Robbins Center's dance studio upstairs, while Alcott Fish, Ashleigh, Ravi, Chris, and Erin worked on their big jealousy number on the stage. Yolanda and Parr needed me to stand in for Alcott, who had a couple of lines in their scene.

To my surprise, Yolanda seemed to be having some trouble remembering her part. Suspicious, I checked her hair. The day before, she had worn all green beads, and her sister wore all red. Today Yolanda still wore green. And the beads weren't just at the ends of her braids, but up at her scalp as well. If this was Yvette in disguise, the twins must have gone to a great deal of trouble to make her look right.

The green beads clicked as my friend leaned her head back for the big reconciliation kiss. I flinched as usual, but forced myself to watch.

Parr kissed her.

"You're not Yolanda, are you?" he said.

She made a gesture of surprise. "Who else would I be?"

"The famous identical twin, maybe?"

"Why do you say that?"

"Yolanda kisses differently. You can tell a lot from a kiss."

The Gerard twin hesitated, then took a deep breath. "You're right," she said. "I'm Yvette."

"I thought so!" I said. "You were so quiet in the car. Where's Yolanda?"

"She got grounded."

"Grounded! What for?"

"Dumb girl says she accidentally ordered some sexy underwear over the Internet, and my mom got the bill. Tell me, how do you *accidentally* order some sexy underwear? She's grounded for two weeks, and she's afraid she'll lose the part if anybody here finds out. You won't tell, will you?"

I shook my head. "Of course not," I said. "Ashleigh's going to notice, though. You should tell her—she'd never give you away."

"Yeah, I wanted to tell you both, but Landa said to wait and see if you noticed. You won't tell either, right?" she asked Parr.

"No, of course not. You know the part—they'd have to replace Yolanda with somebody anyway, so why not you? Why *do* you know it, anyway?"

"I learned it helping my sister practice. Thank you so much, guys. Yolanda will appreciate it."

"I don't get it. I thought you hated performing and things like that," I said.

"Yeah, I do. She owes me."

"You're a generous sister," said Parr. "Shall we take it from after the kiss?"

❧

Except for Parr, Ashleigh, me, and Ned, whom Ash told but swore to secrecy, no one involved with *Insomnia* noticed the new actress playing Tanya. The substitution did have one dramatic result, however. Igsome Chris followed Yvette into the prop room, where she'd gone to put away some test tubes. He yelped and came out again quickly.

"What did you do to him, Yv—Yo?" asked Ashleigh.

"Something my sister should have done weeks ago. That girl's too soft-hearted."

She refused to say more.

Chapter 14

*Musings about the Inscrutable Gender ∽ A Date ∽
Ashleigh to the rescue ∽ Painful Praise.*

When I began tenth grade, I never imagined I would become a Belle, but when Seth Young called the third December evening in a row and Mom made a comment about boys, I began to rethink my self-image.

"It's not *boys*, Mom—it's just Seth. He wanted the math homework."

"The math homework, eh? What did he want yesterday?"

"How do you know he called yesterday? Did you go snooping in my Calls Received list?"

Mom looked hurt. "You know I wouldn't do that. But if he calls you while we're in the car, I can't help overhearing, can I?"

"Well, if you did overhear, you'd know he wanted to find out if I'd finished reading Mad Alex's story for *Sailing*—the literary magazine."

"And the day before?"

"Oh, Mom! It's just Seth. Really—would *you* go out with him?"

"I don't know, honeybear, I don't think I've met him. Unless, is he that nice-looking young man who gave you that chocolate turkey?"

Was he? Whatever Ashleigh might believe about Ned, I hadn't solved the chocolate-turkey mystery to my satisfaction. "I'm not sure," I said. "There's a bunch of people it could be. You didn't exactly give us a good description."

"There, what did I tell you?" said Mom triumphantly. "Boys!"

⤜◦⤛

Taken one by one, I felt, Ned, Igsome Chris, Seth, and Parr added up to something less than—or at least other than—Boys. None of them seemed to be behaving like a real suitor. No matter what Ashleigh said, I couldn't believe that Ned had feelings for me. Igsome did pursue me pointedly—he was out for conquest—but as long as he didn't conquer me, you could say I'd won. However, my victory was nothing personal, as Yvette had shown; he chased after anything female. Nor did Seth fit the bill, I told myself. Nothing could be more natural than for a guy to call a girl with whom he shared several classes and endless literary duties.

As for Parr—well, what was there to say about Parr? I was afraid my conflicted feelings for him might be clouding my observations. The warm, teasing gallantry that marked our first meeting had given way to something more restrained. Now when we were together, I always felt a barrier between us, as if he were quietly holding me off or holding himself back. At moments I even imagined that he was aiming some intensity directly at me, but stopping, perfect swordsman that he was, with the point at my heart, a fraction of an inch from drawing blood. What this meant for Ashleigh and her dreams, I couldn't say. I often thought he treated her with the same courtesy he gave me, but with more freedom, more warmth.

Individually, then, none of these boys seemed to justify that remark of my mother's. Taken all together, though, there certainly were a lot of them. Was Mom right? Did they count as Boys?

∽

There was no talking to Ashleigh about it, of course—I knew I'd just get an earful about Ned. But Sam, when I consulted her, sided with Mom.

"Why does Seth have to call you on the phone about the homework and stuff?" she asked. "If all he wants is information, he could just as easily e-mail you. With the phone, he can get you to give him one-on-one, person-to-person alone time—even if he can't actually get you alone in person. I don't know, Julie. Unless you do something definite to discourage him, I bet he'll make a move soon."

As usual, Samantha was right.

Seth sent me a text message one Thursday afternoon: *can u meet me at java jail 2 discuss page proofs?*

I should have guessed what was going on when he paid for my latte and insisted with extra-nervous pompousness that half my *which*s should have been *that*s, but it wasn't until he had put away all his papers and turned the subject to the movie playing at the Cinepalace that I realized what he had in mind.

"Well, if you haven't seen it either, you want to go see it now?" asked Seth.

"I—I can't—I have to—my mom needs me to help her in the shop," I garbled, taken by surprise.

"Then what about tomorrow night?"

A movie alone with Seth—on a Friday night! What would that mean—what would that make us? What would people think if they saw us?

"I promised Ashleigh," I began, meaning to finish the sentence, "that I'd go see it with her." But I realized in time that I'd already told Seth all about her reaction to the movie, which she'd seen with Emily Mehan the previous weekend, while I was at my Dad's. ". . . that I'd hang out with her and help her with her dance routine," I finished lamely.

Seth got a stubborn look in his face, centered mostly around the jaw. "What about Saturday night, then?" he said.

Saturday night—even worse. I caved. "I'll call my mom and see if I can help her tomorrow instead," I said.

His jaw relaxed and he gave me a proud smile, as if he had beaten me by seven points on an English test and I had praised him for it.

❧

Have you ever been to the movies with a boy you most certainly don't Like? A boy whose hands you can almost feel thinking (as if they had their own separate little brains) about creeping over to your shoulder or reaching for your hands? He leans closer to whisper some sardonic comment to show he's superior to the movie. You nod abruptly, trying to fend him off with your famously pointy chin. His shoulder brushes yours, and you feel him trembling a little under his pose. You draw away to the other side of your seat, pushing against the armrest until it digs into your waist.

I escaped to the ladies' halfway through and put in a rescue call to Ashleigh. "Help," I whispered. "I seem to be on some sort of horrible date or something with Seth Young. Can you meet me accidentally at the Cinepalace in an hour, when the movie gets out?"

"A what? A *date*? With *who*? What?"

"Can't talk now—I've got to get back to my seat—please, it's important—Cinepalace, one hour."

Seth seemed relieved when I came back; I think he was afraid I'd walked out on him altogether. But he bristled when we ran into Ashleigh and the Gerard twins on our way out of the theater, just as he was reaching for my arm.

"Julie! There you are!" cried Ashleigh. "Where were you? We've been trying to call you."

"Where does it look like she was?" said Seth. "We went to see the movie."

"Oh, hi, Seth," said Ashleigh, as if she'd only just noticed him.

"How did you like the movie?" said a twin.

"What are you doing out? I thought you were grounded," I answered. Unsure which one was Yolanda, I directed my question to the space between them.

The one on the left answered. "I got a ninety on my math test from Mr. Klamp, so my mom let me out for the evening. Kind of like bail, or is it parole? We're going to the Java Jail to celebrate. Want to come?"

"We already spent hours there," said Seth. He turned to me, shutting them out with his shoulder. "Shall we go to Bennie's Burgers?" he suggested.

"Yeah, Bennie's, that sounds great," said Ashleigh. Ignoring Seth's irritated look, she took me by the arm and charged off down the street.

❧

"What do you expect, the way you encourage him?" said Yvette later, when we were back at Ashleigh's. Seth had made an

attempt to outwait my friends at the restaurant, but after Ashleigh had shown that she was prepared to out-outwait him, he
had given up and gone home.

"I don't encourage him—what do you mean?" I objected.

"You're always replying to his messages right away and letting him sit next to you in the Nettle's class."

"But what am I supposed to do, without being totally rude?
And how do you know where he sits? You're not even *in*
that class."

Yvette just smiled.

"Well, I am, and she's right—he *is* always sitting next to
you," said Yolanda. "Why don't you like him back, anyway? He
seems like a pretty nice guy, and he's cute too. Not crisp-cute, like
Adam or Ravi, but sort of cutish-cute. He's got that artistic, romantic thing going on. He's got a nice nose. He looked really
good that time at Halloween when he was a pirate. You really
don't like him? I would, if he liked *me* like he likes *you*."

"Landa, your standards are so low," said her sister. "You think
everybody's kind of cute, even when they're igsome. You should
be slapping them yourself, so I don't have to."

"I don't know that Seth is igsome, exactly," I said. "I just don't
Like him."

"The point isn't whether he's igsome," said Ashleigh. "The
point is that Julie's affections are Otherwise Engaged."

"Oh, right, I forgot, you're going out with Ned, right?" said
Yolanda. "But I bet you could still go out with Seth too, if you
wanted. How's Ned going to find out? He doesn't exactly get
out much."

That raised Ashleigh's fighting spirit. "Yolanda! How can you
suggest such a thing?" she flashed out. "Julie would never be so

false—she would never treat anyone with such disloyalty, especially not a noble being like Ned! Her love, like her nature, is pure and true!"

"But I keep telling you, I'm not going out with Ned," I protested feebly. I didn't press the point, though. For one thing, it was useless—I knew I would never change Ashleigh's mind. And her passionate words distracted me, filling me with guilt. Never false—incapable of disloyalty—my nature pure and true. This—from the girl whose hoped-for boyfriend I couldn't get out of my mind! Ashleigh's words would be far, far more fitting if she applied them to herself. How would I ever deserve my loyal friend's praise?

Chapter 15

Holiday cheer ∽ The baby's birthday ∽
Sweet Sixteen and Never Been Kissed ∽ my First Kiss.

The Christmas vacation arrived in a flurry of exams and term papers. The winter issue of *Sailing to Byzantium* went to the printer. Seth dropped off the disk; I used my last English paper as an excuse not to go with him. I rushed through my essay, repeating ideas from the previous one, but Ms. Nettleton didn't notice.

Yolanda's sentence ended, but she got regrounded for cutting physics to hang out with Adam.

Ashleigh and I exchanged our yearly Hanumas/Chrisukka presents. She gave me a CD of songs popular in nineteenth-century parlors—"What Jane Austen's heroines would have listened to instead of musicals," she explained. I made her a magic kit from unsold odds and ends in my mother's shop: a bouquet of colorful scarves, a wand cut down from a broken walking stick, a stuffed rabbit. I was particularly proud of the top hat, which I fitted out with a false bottom and a hinged trapdoor on top. I hoped the gift would spark a new craze—but no. "How Jane Austen's characters would love this!" cried Ashleigh. "Perfect for those long evenings at Pemberley. Hey, what do you think about doing a musical version of *Pride and Prejudice*? Wouldn't this hat look great on Darcy?"

The other major holiday of the season is, of course, my birthday: December 17. It fell early in the vacation, as it usually does. With his strict attention to his parental rights, my father insists on my spending alternate birthdays at each house; this year was his turn.

I awoke to the sound of footsteps on the ceiling of my basement bedroom. The Irresistible Accountant was in the kitchen directly overhead, stomping and crashing breakfast into life. I buried my head in the pillow, but sleep had fled, so I put on my bathrobe and slippers and went upstairs.

Amy handed me a plate of winter-squash frittata, herbed home fries, and sliced citrus salad. "There you are, sweetie," she said. "Happy birthday." Then she burst into tears and ran out of the room.

As I stared after her, my father gestured at my plate with his fork. "Aren't you going to eat your breakfast?" he asked. "Go on, eat it. You'll hurt Amy's feelings."

I took a halfhearted bite. "What's the matter with her? Is my birthday such a tragedy it makes a grown woman cry?"

Dad gave me a look of grave reproach. "How can you be so thoughtless? Don't you know what day it is today?" he said.

"Um, December 17th?"

"Yes, to you it's December 17th—but to Amy, it's the baby's birthday."

"What baby's birthday? She doesn't have a baby."

"That's why she's so upset," said my father patiently. "The baby was due on December 17th. If she hadn't had the miscarriage, today would be his birthday."

I did some arithmetic. "How can that possibly be?" I said. "She had the miscarriage in October. She didn't even look pregnant. The baby can't have been due for months and months."

"Not that miscarriage, Julie," said my father with a touch of irritation, as if I had missed a very easy question on a quiz. "That was only the latest one. You don't know how hard things have been for Amy. I'm talking about the first miscarriage, the one four years ago, when Amy and I first got together. After we lost that baby, she was devastated. Don't you remember? She's been very, very brave, but when we lost the new baby again two months ago, it opened the wound all over again for her. You'll be kind to her today, won't you? I know you will. It's a very sad day for her, and she's feeling very vulnerable."

With these words, my father finished his frittata, put on his coat, and went off to work.

I stared blankly at the elaborate eggs congealing on my plate. After a while, I noticed that my brain had continued to do arithmetic all by itself. The sum it produced horrified me. If my father was telling the truth—and there was no reason to think he wasn't—then Amy had already been pregnant for months before my father left my mother. All those weeks when my parents went together to marriage counseling, all those weeks when he swore to her—and me!—that he would start fresh: all of it lies. He had known all along he would leave. He hadn't meant a word of it.

Of course, I had no illusions that my father had succeeded in the new start he had promised to make. How could I? He had left us, hadn't he? But it was another thing to learn that he hadn't even tried.

And another thing entirely to learn it on my sixteenth birthday.

I abandoned my Familial Restraint Fund for good. No amount of imaginary money could ever compensate for this.

My cell phone rang. I checked the number: my mother, doubtless calling to wish me a happy birthday. I decided I couldn't deal and let the voice mail get it.

Amy came back into the kitchen. "What's the matter, sweetie?" she said. "You're not eating. Don't you like your frittata?"

⟡

With the house already dank with Amy's tears, I balked at adding mine. It was too cold out for long woodland rambles, however, so I took refuge in the Lius' greenhouse next door. The conservatory, I called it in my head. But unlike the conservatory at Forefield—an elegant structure where cast-iron frets offered up crystal panes to the sun—the Lius' version was small and practical, close cousin to a shed. Haichang had built it from plywood and sheet plastic to keep the worst of the cold off his orchids and Lily's vegetables.

It was chilly but bright in the greenhouse. The sun wavered in through the plastic and the thin winter clouds. Carefully moving aside two pots of hybrid phalaenopsis, I sat on a bench, breathed in the wet air, and gave myself over to self-pity.

The worst of it was, I felt I had no real right to feel sorry for myself. I had friends, I had parents (two sets of them) who neither beat nor neglected me, I had good grades, acceptable looks, absorbing activities—all the trappings, I told myself, of privilege. I had my heart's sister, Ashleigh. I even had a suitor, of sorts—not, alas, the guy of my dreams—just Seth. Imagine kissing Seth. Ig! But what if I couldn't escape it? I was getting older and older, and Seth was the closest I had ever come to anything approaching a boyfriend. Sixteen years old already, of all pathetic things! What if my longed-for first kiss was with Seth?

I began to cry in earnest.

The wind ruffling the plastic, the hum of the heater, the gurgle of the humidifier, and my own snuffling sobs filled my ears, so I didn't notice that I was no longer alone until I felt an arm around my shoulder.

"Stringbean! What's the matter?" said a man's voice. Zach, home from college for the vacation. He used an ancient nickname that I'd hoped everyone had forgotten long ago.

"Oh, Zach," I said. "It's my birthday." I hid my face against his shoulder and sobbed harder.

"But Beano, that's a *good* thing. Happy birthday! Seventeen?"

I shook my head, his sweater scratchy against my cheek. "Sixteen," I said.

"Even better! Sweet sixteen."

I sobbed still harder. "Yeah, right. Sweet sixteen and never been kissed."

"Oh, is *that* the problem? Have you really never been kissed? What's the matter with that boyfriend of yours—that Foureyes boy? They're all wimps at that place. Except my young sparring partner Parr, of course, there's a kid with a spine—I bet he's not leaving your little friend Ashleigh unkissed. Hey, easy there, Bean Cuisine, you sound like you're choking. Just because your boyfriend is too scared to make a move, that isn't any reflection on *you*."

"If you mean Ned, he's not my boyfriend," I said for the millionth time. "I know Ashleigh says so, but he isn't. I don't have a boyfriend. And I'm so tall, and I have stringy arms and stringy legs and stringy hair and a stringy face, and nobody ever wanted to kiss me except creeps and stuffy Seth Young, and even if they did, I wouldn't know how."

"Wow," said Zach. "That sounds pretty bad." He held me in his scratchy arms and patted me a little too hard between the shoulder blades, as if he were trying to dislodge a chicken bone. I started to feel a bit better.

"I could show you, if you want," he said. "You could practice on me."

"What do you mean? Practice what?"

"How to kiss. That way when the boy who isn't your boyfriend finally gets off his ass and kisses you, you won't worry about getting it wrong. And if he doesn't—well, anyway, you won't be sweet sixteen and never been kissed."

I took my face out of his sweater and looked at him.

"But not if you don't want to, of course," he said. "Sorry, I didn't mean—"

Quickly, before I could change my mind, I kissed Zach. Handsome Zach, heartthrob of the seniors, kind, vain, teasing, brotherly, out-of-my-league Zach.

❧

The first kiss—the one I launched—landed hard and sudden, off center. I didn't quite know what to do with it. "Mmmm," said Zach tactfully when it was over, taking my face in his hands and moving in with gentle expertise.

"That's the way," he said when he was done. "Another?"

I nodded. This time our mouths came open a little. Alarmed, I felt myself fluttering. Something bumped, something seemed to tangle.

"Easy, now," said Zach, pulling back. "Relax."

I nodded again. After the next kiss, it began to feel almost natural—more like a dance, and less like two people trying to push through the same swinging door from opposite sides. I found I could even breathe while kissing; I considered opening my eyes. Before I could, however, I felt a crash judder through Zach's torso, bumping his teeth into mine. "Ow!" he said.

Simultaneously, I heard Samantha yell: "Zach! You creep! Leave her alone! What are you doing?"

I opened my eyes. Sam was hitting Zach with a bag of potting soil. I had never seen her so angry.

"Julie! Are you okay? Zach, what do you think you're doing?"

"What does it look like I'm doing?" answered Zach, brushing soil off his jeans.

"It's okay, Sam," I said, mortified. "*I* kissed *him*."

Samantha looked at me for a moment, then turned back to Zach. "How can you be so irresponsible?" she said. "What about Jenna?"

"Calm down, Sam. You don't need to throw dirt around. I'm not cheating on Jenna, it's just a kiss. Julie and I both know what we're doing. It's her birthday and she was feeling lonely. Nobody's going to get their heart broken. Julie's in love with that Forefield boy, anyway."

Samantha put the bag of potting soil down. "Get out of here, Zach," she said. "I mean it, go on." Zach gave me a sheepish look, brushed off more dirt, and left. Sam turned to me. "I apologize for Zach—he's an idiot," she said. "Are you all right?"

Was I? I had no idea how I felt—thrilled, terrified, shaken? I needed to go away somewhere and figure it out, but first I needed to calm Sam down. "It's okay, Sam," I said. "I'm not going to do anything stupid like fall for Zach. Don't worry about it, okay? He caught me crying and he was comforting me. That's all. He wasn't taking advantage of me. *I* kissed *him*."

"If you say so," said Sam. "But if you need me to kill him, tell me. In fact, I might just do it anyway. Oh, and happy birthday, by the way."

Chapter 16

Paperwhites ✧ Hothouse flowers ✧ The Great White Way ✧
Parr's house ✧ Footprints in the snow ✧ A Third sonnet.

When I got home, I found someone had slipped into my room and cleaned it up for me. My bed was made, my clothes neatly straightened, my collection of shells, stones, bones, and fascinating bits of broken china carefully dusted and arranged on their shelf. The floor gleamed, as if someone had mopped it. There wasn't a cobweb in sight, not even in the farthest reaches of the roof peak, where a displaced spider had begun to spin new tether lines. Even my desk was free of dust, the books and papers arranged in the exact order I had left them in, but with their corners straightened, all at right angles. A bowl of paperwhites bloomed on my windowsill, filling the room with their sweet, slightly gasoliny fragrance.

This, I realized at once, must be Ashleigh's birthday present to me. She knew she was the only person who could get away with touching my things.

Sure enough, her curly head popped up at the window. "Open up," she said. "It's starting to get icy out here."

Looking at my sparkling room and my grinning friend, I felt ashamed of myself. What did I have to complain of, compared with what I had to be thankful for? I pushed the window up and gave Ashleigh a hand in.

"Happy birthday," she announced with satisfaction, taking off her sneakers so as not to track bark dust on the gleaming floor. I noticed that she was wearing jeans, without any regard for the visibility of her lower limbs. "How was it? Did anything earth-shattering happen?"

"Actually, yes," I said. I was tired of keeping secrets from Ashleigh. This, at least, I could tell her. Perhaps she could help me figure out what I had done and why.

"Wait, let me get this straight," said Ashleigh when I was done. "You kissed Zach Liu? Four times?"

"Yes—well, technically, I only kissed him once. The other times *he* kissed *me*."

"But Julie, I had no idea you felt that way about Zach. Why didn't you tell me?"

"Because I *don't* feel 'that way' about him. If you mean am I interested in him, no, I'm not. That would be idiotic. He's way out of my league. All the girls at Byz have a crush on him, and he knows it. He's in college, for God's sake. He has a girlfriend. I'm barely sixteen."

"Then why did you kiss him? What about Ned?"

"What *about* Ned? Ash, come on! I keep telling you. I'm not interested in Ned. I was never interested in Ned. He's a nice guy, but I'm not interested in him. And he's not interested in me, either. He sure as hell never tried to kiss me."

"I see," said Ashleigh. "I wish I hadn't interrupted you guys in the trophy room that time, before he had a chance. I wish I'd just tiptoed out without saying anything! I would have, but I thought I was rescuing you from Chris. Well, I guess I can understand it. You get tired of waiting for the one you love to kiss you, so you go and kiss someone else."

I sighed. She was right, although not the way she thought.

"Do you realize I'm sixteen years old and I never kissed any-one?" I said. "Ned never wanted to kiss me. That's not what we were doing in the trophy room. Nobody ever wanted to kiss me—unless you count Seth, maybe, which I'd rather not. I didn't really know what I was doing when I kissed Zach. I wanted to see what it was like. I guess I was afraid that if I waited, Seth would somehow get me to let him kiss me, with that stubborn persist-ence of his, and then that would be my first kiss. At least Zach is someone I like."

"So he *is* someone you like!"

"Not *Like*—just like. He's a nice guy, he's really good-looking, he's Samantha's big brother, and he's a college student, away in college, where he has a girlfriend. He's not going to be after me to go out with him like Seth is. Anyway, why do I have to Like someone before I can kiss him? Are you in love with Ravi? You kiss *him* every week—twice a week, or more."

"But that's different—I have to, for the play. I wouldn't if I didn't have to."

"Why not? Doesn't Ravi kiss well?"

"I don't know—he's fine, I guess—but I'm not interested in him."

"Well, have you ever kissed Parr, then?" I asked. As soon as I said it, I wished I hadn't.

"No, of course not, you'd know if I had. I would never keep such a thing from you," she said impatiently. "So what *was* it like?"

"What—kissing Zach?"

"Yes."

"It was—nice. Surprisingly nice. I'd do it again in a heart-beat."

"You'd kiss Zach again?" said Ashleigh, shocked. "I thought you said he has a girlfriend!"

"Well, maybe not Zach—Samantha would kill me. Anyway, she'd kill one of us. And there *is* that girlfriend. But somebody, yes, I'd definitely kiss somebody, if it was the right guy."

The likelihood of kissing the Right Guy, however, seemed so distant that I allowed myself to wish, for a moment or two, that Zach was unattached, that he wasn't in college, that he wasn't the son of my father's partner, wasn't as far above me as the reindeer on Ashleigh's roof, and would kiss me again, this time without a dirt-throwing sister to interrupt.

∽

Samantha came by the next day with an armful of flowers. I recognized them from her parents' greenhouse. She made Zach drive her in the famous Saab, but she wouldn't let him get out of the car. "Happy birthday," she said. "These are from my idiot brother. I'm delivering them personally to make sure the message comes through loud and clear. They're not romantic flowers. They're happy-birthday, I'm-sorry-I-molested-you, will-you-ever-forgive-me-or-does-my-sister-have-to-kill-me flowers."

"I wanted to get you roses, but Sam wouldn't let me," called Zach from the car.

"Shut up!" said Sam, and hit him through the window.

∽

For Christmas, Ashleigh's parents gave her a pair of tickets to see *Fascination!* on Broadway, and she invited me. We rode down on the Metro-North train and stayed overnight with my aunt Ruth and uncle John. We spent the afternoon before the show eating dumplings in Chinatown, browsing through the giant used book-store in the Village, and trying on false moustaches at a theatri-cal supply shop.

The best part of the show was the songs. Ashleigh couldn't get over the voices and the orchestration, and I thought the lyrics were almost as clever as Parr's. When the curtain fell, we clapped until our hands went numb.

We slept in Aunt Ruth and Uncle John's living room, Ash-leigh on the couch and me on an inflatable mattress. I sank slowly through my dreams and woke up in the morning flat on the floor, with a crick in my back. "Oh, dear," said Aunt Ruth. "Looks like the bed needs a patch. Sorry about that."

We spent the morning at the Frick Museum, the former Fifth Avenue mansion of a nineteenth-century steel magnate that houses his art collection. We enjoyed ourselves arguing about which of the portraits matched which of the people we knew. Ashleigh was easy: she could have been the model for George Romney's portrait of Lady Hamilton, a pretty young woman in a red dress with abundant dark hair and a lively little dog under her arm. It was harder to find a picture of me, though. Ashleigh pointed to a graceful Gainsborough lady in an elaborate blue dress, but I felt more like a severe Whistler girl in black.

After lunch Ashleigh said, "Hey, doesn't Grandison Parr live in this neighborhood? Let's go check out his house. Maybe Ned will be there too."

"I don't know, Ash," I said. I felt the familiar dread of public embarrassment. "What will we say if they see us? And why would Ned be there, anyway?"

"We'll say we were in the neighborhood, which is true. And Ned told me he'd be spending some of the vacation with the

Parrs. Come on." She pulled my arm over her shoulder with both her hands and used it to tug me down the street.

"Okay, okay, let go," I said. Recovering my arm, I followed her with a sigh.

Parr turned out to live in a tall, narrow town house that looked as if it had been built around the same time as the Frick Museum, a century or so ago. It had a limestone stoop leading up to a shiny red door. My heart fluttered to think that I was looking at his home, where he read, showered, slept, dreamed.

My heart fluttered even more—in a very bad way—when Ashleigh started up the stairs to ring the doorbell. I hauled her back. "No. Absolutely not. People don't just ring each other's doorbells around here." She protested, but I refused to let go. "If you do, I'm leaving without you. I'll catch the early train back. I'm serious, Ashleigh."

"Oh, all right," she said. She leaned against a tree on the sidewalk in front and looked up. "Which window do you think is his? Do you think Ned is staying in the guest room? Which window do you think is the guest room?"

The thought that Parr might be standing behind one of those windows—might look out and see us—sent scared thrills buzzing in my wrists. "I don't know," I said. "You've seen where he lives, okay? Can we go now?"

"Just hang on a minute—maybe they'll come out."

"If they do, I'll die of embarrassment. Come on, let's go. It's cold out here. I feel like an idiot."

"Well, if you let me ring the doorbell, we could go in and get warm," said Ashleigh.

"Good-bye, I'm leaving now, see you back in Byzantium," I said.

"Okay, okay, okay! Just wait a little. Maybe they'll come out."
Fortunately, they didn't.

A tall blonde girl walked by slowly, looking at the windows. "Do you think that's that girlfriend of Parr's?" I whispered.

"What girlfriend?"

"That Sam's friend was talking about—remember, in the e-mail?"

"Could be. I'll go ask her—maybe she knows where they are," said Ashleigh.

"Ashleigh, you're nuts! Don't you dare," I hissed, holding her arm as tightly as I could. The girl walked away down the block.

After half an hour of stamping in the cold, even Ashleigh admitted her feet were getting numb. We caught the 2:25 north from Grand Central.

~*~

The weather turned bitter after New Year's. Drafts slashed through my attic. They were more painful than usual because my mother and I had decided to keep the thermostat low, to save on heating oil. I piled every available blanket on the bed and took to sleeping in my warmest, ugliest pajamas, the ones with fried eggs on them. I even wore a cap to bed.

Snow fell: not enough to shut the schools, alas, but enough to add half an hour of shoveling to our mornings. Our tree grew damp and awkward, liable to dump snow down our necks. Ashleigh and I suspended our arboreal crossings until kinder weather.

School started again. In history, the French revolutionaries stormed the Bastille. In English, we began reading *Pride and Prejudice*, to my dismay—I worried the Nettle would ruin my favorite book. Ashleigh and Yolanda did their best by raising their hands nonstop and talking as long as possible whenever she called on them. For once, though, Seth's class participation fell. He's one of those boys who consider Jane Austen silly and trivial. He did have a few nice things to say about Elizabeth's father, Mr. Bennet, whom he found witty, in contrast to the "repellent" Mr. Darcy.

The Forefielders returned to their palace on the hill. Ashleigh got e-mail from Ned saying they were back. He had indeed spent his vacation with the Parrs, but on Bermuda, not in Manhattan, so I had wasted all my anxiety on East 74th Street. *Insomnia* rehearsals didn't start up yet, however—the boys had their finals after their vacation, poor things, and extracurriculars were suspended so they could study.

"Did you hear anything last night, Julie?" asked Ashleigh one morning as we waited for the school bus.

"What kind of anything?"

"Sort of thrashing. I thought it was a bear, or a deer eating the tree, but when I looked in the morning, I saw footprints in the snow. People feet, not deer hoofs. Unless the deer was wearing boots."

"Do you think it was a person eating the tree?"

"People don't usually like bark, do they?"

"Not unless it's almond bark."

We paused for a moment of nostalgia, remembering the many delicious pounds of almond bark we had made during Ashleigh's candy-making period.

"Funny, I wonder who it was," said Ashleigh.

There were no more footprints when we checked for the next couple of days, but three days later—a Saturday—we found the snowdrift beneath our tree kicked and dented. Not only that, but pinned to the tree with a red thumbtack was a sonnet, its edges curling from the damp. Fortunately, it had been written in ballpoint, so the ink hadn't run.

This is what it said:

Just let me wait a little while longer
Under your window in the quiet snow.
Let me stand here and shiver. I'll be stronger
If I can see your light before I go.
All through the weeks I've tried to keep my balance.
Leaves fell, then rain, then shadows. I fell, too.
Easy restraint is not among my talents;
Fall turned to winter and I came to you.
Kissed by the snow, I contemplate your face.
O do not hide it in your pillow yet!
Warm rooms would never lure me from this place
If only I could see your silhouette.
Turn on your light, my sun, my summer love.
Zero degrees down here: July above.

"Wow!" said Ashleigh. "Somebody likes you!"

"Why me? It could just as easily be you."

"He tacked it to your side of the tree."

"That's the easiest side to reach."

"But it's obviously about you, Julie! He even uses your name. Look, 'July above.' Not quite Julie, but close enough. And he says, 'Easy restraint is not among my talents.' If that's not Ned describing himself, I don't know what it is. He's so sincere—so spontaneous—so unrestrained!"

"I disagree—it doesn't sound like Ned to me," I said. "That's not how he writes. He misspells like crazy, and he doesn't use punctuation—at least, in e-mail he doesn't. If I were going to guess, I'd say it's Parr. We know he likes to rhyme. Doesn't *pillow yet/silhouette* sound like some of the *Insomnia* lyrics? And *balance/talents*?"

"Parr? I guess that's possible. Does *Parr* like you too? Ned *and* Parr? Well, I don't blame them a bit!"

Parr! Writing love poems to *me*? Could it be possible? And was there pain in Ashleigh's voice as she suggested it? I hastened to reassure her. "No, no, Ash, he's clearly talking about you," I said. "Listen: 'My sun, my summer love.' That's got to be you, you're much sunnier than me."

"No, silly, that's you, you're the sunny one—I'm dark and curly. Could it be Seth? He writes for that literary magazine of yours, and we know for a fact that he likes you."

"Oh, I hope not! I don't think so, though. He thinks he's Emerson, not Shakespeare."

We debated for a while longer without resolving the question. Ashleigh, generous girl—stubborn girl—insisted that I take the sonnet home with me. I pinned it on my bulletin board beside the other mysterious note, the one from the chocolate turkey. I studied them, trying to decide whether the same person had written them both. The turkey note was cramped and messier, possibly because the writer had to fit his message on the side of a small box, but the letters seemed not dissimilar. I decided I needed a larger handwriting sample from the turkey giver before I could say for sure.

Chapter 17

A Limited Junior License ⌒ A disastrous Mocharetto ⌒
Mint Sauce ⌒ My father and stepmother Approve.

Seth Young stopped me as I was leaving school with Ashleigh and the Gerards that Tuesday. "Oh, Julie, Ms. Nettleton says the printer called," he said. "The bound copies of *Sailing* are ready. Eleanor asked me to pick them up. Can you come help? It's over in North Byz."

It seemed impossible to refuse without being rude. "All right—how are we getting there? Is Ms. Nettleton driving us?"

"No," he said proudly, "I am. I got my license last week."

"Don't you need an adult in the car till you're eighteen?"

"Nope—Limited Junior License: may drive alone for school course or activity. This is a school activity."

I gave Ashleigh a help-me look. "Great!" she said. "North Byz—that's where Yv and Yo live. You can take the three of us with you and drop us off."

Seth gave her a look of fake concern. "Sorry, Ashleigh, I wish I could, but it's a Limited Junior License. No more than two underage passengers."

I tried a last-ditch effort to discourage him. "I better call my dad and see if it's okay. I'm not sure he'll want me driving with someone who just got his license last week."

"Let me talk to him, then," said Seth.

Worse and worse.

Terri, Dad's receptionist, put me through. "Dad, is it okay if I come home a little late? I need to go with my friend Seth to pick up the bound copies of *Sailing to Byzantium*. The literary magazine, remember? He'll be driving—he got his driver's license last week."

Dad expressed concern, as I'd hoped he would.

"Yes, just last week. I don't know, I've never seen him drive, but I'm sure it'll be fine, he's very energetic," I said in an attempt to alarm my father further while making Seth think I was calming him down.

Seth tugged on my arm to ask for the phone. "Hang on," I told Dad, "he wants to talk to you."

"Hello, Dr. Lefkowitz?" said Seth. "Seth Young. I just wanted to assure you that I'm a very safe driver and I'll take good care of your daughter. I had sixty hours of practice before I took my road test—twice the recommended state guidelines. I got perfect scores on all the exams, including the road test. I'm certified in first aid and CPR. Not that I expect them to be necessary this afternoon, of course, but I think it speaks to my character. What? Yes, my parents' Volvo. . . . No, never. . . . Of course. . . . Oh, that sounds wonderful, thank you very much, I'll just have to ask my parents." He handed me the phone back. "He wants to talk to you again."

"Your friend sounds like a very responsible young man," said my father. "I invited him to dinner. Amy's roasting a leg of lamb."

❧

Seth drove exactly at the speed limit the whole way to the printer, coming to a complete stop at every stop sign. He held the steering wheel with both hands and checked his mirrors five times a minute.

We handed over our paperwork in the storefront office and sat down to wait on the mahogany-red vinyl sofa. Seth draped his arm along the back, a little too close to me, but not quite close enough that I could shrug it off. I stood up and wandered around the room to look at the framed handbills hanging on the walls, samples of the printer's work. After a few minutes, we heard the thumping trundle of our order approaching on a dolly.

"Here you go, kids," said the printer. "There's your disk back, and your receipt."

Seth insisted on opening a box and inspecting a copy of the magazine. He flipped through it, snapping the pages to feel the weight of the paper, and studied the cover picture through a magnifying frame he found on the counter. I couldn't help rolling my eyes.

The printer winked at me. "Everything look okay?" he asked Seth.

Seth completed his inspection. "It's all good," he pronounced.

We rolled the boxes out to the car, Seth pulling, me steadying, the dolly doing its best to make a break for it, and loaded them into the trunk. They were heavier than they looked. "Bend from the knees," instructed Seth. "Use your legs, not your back."

On the way back to school, I made up my mind to find out whether Seth was responsible for the sonnet on the tree. I hoped not, but if so, perhaps there was more to him than I thought.

"Seth, have you ever written a sonnet?" I asked.

"Oh, yes, several. I had one in the issue before last of *Sailing*— don't you remember? My most recent was for Ms. Nettleton's class, for the creative writing assignment in October. It was about moral responsibility. Why do you ask? Are you writing one? Would you like me to read it and give you advice? It's a tricky form, but I'm sure you can learn."

Seth, I concluded with a silent sigh of relief, could not be our secret arboreal author. Last weekend's sonnet, with its references to snow, must have been written more recently than October, and if Seth *had* written it, he would have made sure I knew.

After we unloaded the boxes in the English Department office—Seth had Ms. Nettleton's elevator key, a sign of supreme favor—he asked, "Want to stop at the Java Jail? It's only four-thirty, so we have plenty of time before your dad expects us. Come on, let's get a mocharetto. This is cause for celebration!"

"All right," I said reluctantly. "Just one."

The Java Jail was crowded when we got there. I grabbed the only table left, a tippy, drafty one near the door, while Seth went to order.

Looking around, I saw with alarm that most of the customers were boys in Forefield uniforms. What if someone I knew saw me with Seth?

He came back with our steaming drinks. "Here you go." He moved his chair closer to mine and lifted his paper cup in its dimpled cardboard sleeve. "A toast: to *Sailing*, the magazine that brought us together!"

As I lifted my cup in return, I felt a cold blast run down my neck. Foreboding? Air from outside? It seemed rude not to return the toast. But I couldn't quite bear to meet Seth's eyes, so I turned mine away—and met, instead, the eyes of Grandison Parr, standing at the door.

"Hello, Julia," said Parr, with a formal smile.

"Parr! What are—I thought you guys had finals."

"They ended today. We get the afternoon out to blow off steam."

Seth cleared his throat.

"Oh! I'm sorry," I said. "Seth Young—Grandison Parr. Seth—Seth and I—we work on the literary magazine—he's in my English class—we just . . ." I trailed off.

"How do you do?" said Seth stiffly, offering his hand, as if he expected a Forefield boy to have fancy manners and wanted to prove that his were just as good.

Parr took his hand and shook it. "A pleasure. Well, don't let me interrupt." He gave me another formal smile and moved on into the café.

Should I have asked him to join us? But I wouldn't have been able to bear it, having Parr see Seth at his most pompous, having Parr think that this was the sort of person I would choose to associate with. My mocharetto scorched my mouth. I edged my chair around so that I had my back to Parr. For the duration of our drinks, I felt my back burning like a sacked and fallen city.

❧

Naturally, my father was pulling into the garage just as Seth and I drove up. He stood at the door and watched Seth perform a perfect, though unnecessary, parallel parking maneuver.

"Come on in," he said. "Seth, I presume? You're staying to dinner, right?"

"Oh, yes, thanks," said Seth, stepping out of the car and following Dad into the house.

"Amy, this is Julie's friend Seth," said my father.

"Nice to meet you, Mrs. Lefkowitz," said Seth.

"Hello, Seth. I'm glad you can stay," said the Irresistible.

"There's plenty of food—I roasted a leg of lamb." She turned to me. "And I made that mint sauce you like, sweetie, with fresh mint from the Lius' greenhouse."

The thought of the Lius' greenhouse, on top of everything else, made my stomach lurch.

While I struggled to eat dinner, Seth regaled Dad and Amy with details of our *Sailing* responsibilities and my improvement in Ms. Nettleton's eyes since I'd taken them on. I watched my father and stepmother inflating with approval, like Aunt Ruth's air mattress. (I wondered how soon, also like the air mattress, it would all leak out again.)

"Seth," I said when dinner was over, "don't you have to get going? Doesn't the Limited Junior License come with a curfew?"

"Yes, you're right: 9 P.M.," said Seth reluctantly. "Thanks for dinner, Mrs. Lefkowitz—it was delicious. Julie? Walk me to the car?"

Dinner with my folks had clearly boosted his confidence. He looked as though he might try to kiss me once my father and Amy were out of sight. "No shoes," I said, wiggling my toes in his direction. I stayed firmly seated and let Amy show him out.

"Thanks again, Mrs. Lefkowitz. See you tomorrow, Julie."

"What a nice young man! Good-looking too," said Amy after the door shut. "You sly girl, is *that* why you joined the literary magazine! Why didn't you tell us?"

Chapter 18

My first appearance in Print ∽ Ashleigh interferes ∽
A Midnight Visitor ∽ A Quatrain.

Ashleigh loyally bought four copies of *Sailing*: one for herself, one for each of her parents, and one, she said, for Ned. Although it would have been the depths of ingratitude to ask her not to, I wished she hadn't. The editorial board had chosen a poem of mine that I now felt was perhaps a trifle too personal—too open to interpretation—too revealing. They had published it under my initials, not my full name, but I was afraid that anyone who knew me would easily figure out what they stood for. Indeed, Ashleigh already had. I'll spare you the details, but if you want to get the flavor, imagine what a girl of some sensitivity might have written in her first flush of excitement at meeting the person who was to become the Magnet of Her Thoughts.

Plus, the rhymes were pretty lame.

"I don't think it's lame at all! I think it's beautiful!" insisted Ashleigh, handing over the nineteen dollars. "A fitting tribute to—all right, all right, don't hit me. I won't say it. But I still don't see why you won't admit it. Your poem's about a million times better than Seth's three essays, anyway—*yours* is sincere. Speaking of which, sorry I couldn't chaperone you yesterday. How did it go?"

"Oh, my God, Ash, it was awful! He somehow managed to charm Dad into inviting him to dinner, and now he thinks he's my boyfriend."

"How can he?"

"He clearly thinks it's like getting your driver's license, or A's in math, or getting the Nettle to like you. You just follow the steps right, and that's it, you're done."

"What if you told him you already have a boyfriend?"

"Oh, I don't know—I thought about it—but I *don't* have a boyfriend. I can't quite bring myself to just lie straight out."

"It's not actually so much of a lie. At the rate you're going, you will soon."

"At the rate I'm going, if I do, it'll be Seth. But it's weird, isn't it? I really don't get it. What is it about me? If *I* were a guy, I wouldn't look at me twice. I'm so tall and gawky."

"Don't say those things about my best friend! You're beautiful! You look like a model, only not weird. You don't have that overgrown-grasshopper thing. And you're more approachable. You have this quality of agreeableness that guys find . . . well, agreeable. You go along with things. What you need is for the right one to give you something good to go along with."

I saw the Right One quite a bit once the *Insomnia* rehearsals began again—which they did that week, with a vengeance. There were, after all, very few weeks left until February 2, opening night. But he gave me nothing but measured politeness, with the occasional smoldering look.

"Has Ned said anything yet?" asked Ashleigh one evening, absently scratching Juniper behind the ears. He was no longer a kitten, but a rangy young cat. We were doing our homework in her room, which was far better heated than mine.

"Has Ned said anything about what?"

"You know—has he explained himself, has he declared his intentions? I thought he would have by now. I gave him a strong hint last week."

"Ashleigh! You didn't! You . . . What did you say?"

"I told him he'd better get moving if he didn't want to miss his chance, because you had a serious suitor."

"Ash! I'm going to kill you! How could you do that?"

"I'm sorry, but I just couldn't stand it anymore, watching you wait and wait. The suspense was driving *me* nuts too."

"But Ashleigh—I keep telling you—oh, never mind, it's pointless. I think I'm going to die of embarrassment." I buried my head in my hands and moaned. "What did he say?" I asked.

"He didn't say anything. He's as shy as you are. But Parr asked if I meant that guy from the literary magazine. I said yes. How does Parr know Seth? You never told me they'd met."

The humiliation!

I wanted to kill Ashleigh, but of course it wasn't really her fault, since she didn't know how I felt about Parr. I tried to feel glad about that. After all, I had tried as hard as I could to keep it hidden from her. From Parr too. Could he really not know, when I felt so strongly? Surely he would see it in my eyes! Was he treating me with that distant politeness because he knew how I felt and didn't return my feelings? Or did he have no idea what he meant to me? Maybe he did like me, but he thought I was going out with Seth.

Horrible!

I thought about explaining to Parr next time I saw him, but what would I say? That I didn't like Seth—that he wasn't my boyfriend? Any such explanation seemed presumptuous, since it assumed that Parr would care. And anyway, there was still the question of Ashleigh.

Twice during rehearsal breaks I tried to speak, but I couldn't bring myself to do it.

Meanwhile, the *Insomnia* production advanced at breakneck speed. Mr. Hatchek, the Forefield art teacher, set the entire sophomore (or rather, fourth form) art class to work painting backdrops. The costumes were mostly ordinary streetclothes, an exotic sight at Forefield. It took more fuss than you would think possible to get the cast outfitted in scruffy jeans. I began going over to the Gerards' to help Yvette rehearse with Yolanda so Yolanda would be up to speed on her part when her grounding was over. Yolanda even risked showing up for rehearsal once a week, leaving her sister behind to cover for her with their parents. The plan was for each of them to take the part in one of the play's two performances.

∽

Late in January, I woke with a start in the middle of the night. It had snowed heavily the week before. Hip-deep drifts covered the roots of our oak tree, even in its sheltered position between Ashleigh's house and mine. Some large animal must have blundered into the hidden roots and branches; I could hear it crashing around in distress. Pulling the quilt around my shoulders, I opened the window to look.

Snow was falling heavily, obscuring my view, but I could see that it was no deer down there.

"Ashleigh, is that you?" I called softly.

The figure looked up. "Julia?" it said.

"Who's that?"

"It's me—Grandison. I d-didn't mean to wake you."

"Grandison! What are you doing down there?"

"I—I got locked out. I hoped—I th-thought if you w-were awake—"

His teeth were chattering so hard, he could barely talk.

"You're frozen! You'd better come up here. Do you think you can climb up? It's pretty icy. Should I come down and let you in the door?"

"No, d-don't, I've g-got it." He swung himself up from branch to branch with surprising grace. Clumps of snow fell around him and sank into the drift below.

I gave him a hand in and shut the window quickly. His gloves, his sleeves were icy wet. My room, though drier, seemed only a shade warmer than the air outside. He stood shivering by the window, dripping snow on the floor.

Grandison Parr in my room!

Parr in my room, and me in my fried-egg pajamas, my nightcap like something out of "The Night Before Christmas," my hair poking unevenly out of its braid, and my feet in fuzzy pink slippers, a gift from Amy, which I would have thrown away long ago if they weren't the only thing that could protect me from the demonic chill of the floor. I quickly took off my ridiculous nightcap and turned on the light.

We blinked at each other. His face was red and white.

"You're soaked—you better get out of those wet things," I said. I took his coat, hat, and scarf to drip in the storeroom next door. I put his boots up on the drying rack, which was built for apples, and brought him a towel.

"I'm s-s-sorry to b-b-barge in," began Parr. He could hardly talk through his chattering teeth.

"I know, it's freezing in here," I said. I felt his arm; the sleeve of his sweater was wet. "I'll find you some dry clothes." I rummaged in my dresser and came up with clean sweatpants, T-shirt, and sweatshirt. For almost the first time, I was glad to be so tall. "There, I think these should fit. Go in there and put them on."

When he came back from the storeroom, he was still shivering violently. His lips were blue. I handed him my quilt.

"Th-thanks, Julia. I'm s-sorry to burst in on you like this—I didn't mean to wake you."

"What are you doing here, anyway?"

"I—I got locked out of c-campus and it's pretty nasty out there. I didn't know where to go. You're an angel—thanks for the dry clothes. I'll just wait here a little while until it lets up a bit, if you don't mind, and then I'll go back."

"Go back? How will you get in?"

"How?—Oh. There's a place in the wall where I can sometimes get over. I—My hands were too cold when I tried to climb it before, but I'm warmer now."

"Are you serious?" I said. "All the way back to Forefield in this snow—in your wet coat? You'll freeze to death! You'll never get over the wall if you didn't before. They have to unlock the gates in the morning, right? You'd b-better stay here until then."

"Oh, no—now *you're* shivering," he said. "Here, take this back."

He tried to put the quilt around me, but I resisted. "You need it more than I d-do," I said. I couldn't tell whether I was trembling from cold or from his nearness.

"It's big enough for two," he said, wrapping it around both of us.

Parr's icy hand grew warmer on my shoulder. He smelled

beautiful—like wet hair and tree bark and strength. My cheeks burned. I thought they must be giving off enough heat to warm the room—to warm the whole house.

"Julia, I'd better go," said Parr after a while. "I can't stay here all night. You need to sleep. I'll be fine."

The insane gallantry! "No—you will *not* be fine. You'll get frostbite. You're staying here till morning. You can take my bed, and I'll sleep downstairs on the couch."

"If anyone's sleeping on a couch, it's me."

"You can't—my mother will freak if she sees you."

"Won't she wonder why *you're* sleeping on the couch, then?"

I considered this. If Mom caught me sleeping downstairs, she'd die of guilt for keeping the thermostat so low. She'd insist on turning it up for the rest of the winter, which we couldn't afford. But with my room so cold, I didn't have enough blankets for two.

"See? It won't work. Where did you put my boots?" he said.

"I'm not giving them back. You're not going anywhere. We can both sleep here, in my bed."

"Oh, no," Parr protested. "I couldn't do that."

"Don't worry, you'll be perfectly safe. I'll keep my hands to myself," I said.

He opened his mouth, then closed it again. Silently he helped me remake the bed, tucking the quilt in well. I got in; he turned out the light and got in after me, scrunching himself up as far away as possible—which wasn't very far. Our shoulders touched.

"Are you comfortable? Have I left you enough room?" he asked.

"I'm fine."

"You're still shivering. Are you warm enough?"

"Yes, I'm fine. I know it's cold in here, but I'm used to it. What about you—are you warm enough?" Not that there was anything I could do if he wasn't; hold him in my arms, maybe. I shivered and turned toward the wall, leaving his shoulder behind.

"Toasty. Embarrassed, but toasty. Good night, Julia. And thank you."

"Good night, Grandison."

꙼

For a long time we lay at our separate edges of the bed, back to back, the inch between us burning like lava. I felt the blankets move with his breathing. Was he asleep? He couldn't be. What was he thinking? I wanted to turn and put my arms around him and breathe in his smell. I wanted to curl myself into a trembling ball and shrink away to nothing, far, far away from him and everything else, never to emerge again. I wanted the night to last forever, the two of us side by side, with no end and no consequences.

A long time later I woke to find myself strangely warm in my cold room, with warm, steady breaths in my ear. After a moment I remembered who was there. Parr had turned over sometime in the night. He had his arm over my waist, his knees bent behind mine, like a pair of spoons. I felt his chest against my back, rising and falling with his sleeping breath. Blissful, I fell asleep again.

I next woke in the gray of dawn. It had stopped snowing. Parr was standing by my bed, dressed, wearing his boots and holding his coat. "Shh—I didn't mean to wake you again," he whispered.

"What time is it?"

"Six o'clock. The gate should be open by the time I get back."

"You found your boots."

"Yeah, you hid them pretty well, but I found them. Thank you, Julia. You're the best." He smiled that white-and-blue smile of his, bright with the turquoise of his eyes, upheld by his vertical dimple.

"Be careful going down the tree."

"I will." He gently lifted the end of my braid and kissed it, like a gentleman kissing a lady's hand. "Good-bye, Rapunzel."

~o

I woke for the third time an hour later, dreaming I was kissing someone. Was it all a dream, then?

Apparently not. Pinned to my bulletin board, under the sonnet Ashleigh had found on the tree, was a note:

Generous Julia,
Graceful and truly a
Port in a storm:
So calm, so warm.

The handwriting looked familiar. With good reason: it was the same as in the sonnet.

I was right, then. Parr was the mystery poet—Parr had written the sonnet.

But to whom? That was still a mystery. To me? To Ashleigh? If it was to me, I thought with a little laugh, how disappointed he must have been when he got upstairs. "Warm rooms would never lure me from this place," he had written. Well, that was for sure! No warm rooms in this house! And "Zero degrees down here: July above." July—ha! More like February.

Like February in my room, yes; but not in my bed—not in his arms.

Some minutes passed while I stared ahead of me, the hairbrush frozen in my hand, contemplating my bed and his arms.

"Julie! Julie, honey, are you up?" called my mother up the stairs, breaking my reverie. "It's almost eight o'clock."

"Coming, Mom!"

Whoever the sonnet was addressed to, it cast doubt on Parr's explanation of what he was doing under my window. Had he really found himself locked out of Forefield and come here for refuge? Possibly. But he had been downstairs at the foot of our tree at least once before, when he left the sonnet. Wasn't it possible that he had come again last night for the same reason, drawn by the presence of one of us—just as Ashleigh had dragged me to visit *his* house and look up at *his* window over Christmas vacation?

Chapter 19

A song ∽ an Unspeakable Scandal ∽
my Mother takes a new Job ∽ the Talk ∽ a theatrical disaster.

I just made the bus. "Jules, I have a surprise for you," said Ashleigh as we got on.

"What is it?"

"Has it occurred to you that once the play's over, it's no more Forefield for us?"

"Well, yes, it has," I said. It had indeed occurred to me, and today it was almost too painful to bear.

"So Ned and I have been thinking what to do about it, and we came up with a solution. Here!" She produced a piece of paper from her loose-leaf binder and handed it to me proudly.

"What's this?" I said.

"Look at it!"

I did. It was a sheet of music, a song apparently—and the lyrics were my poem from *Sailing*.

"Wow, Ashleigh—did you write this?"

"Yes. Well, mostly. Ned helped."

"Wow! That's amazing." I tried to hum it. I'm not so great at sight-reading; Ashleigh sang it to me. I had to admit, it was a good tune. "That's beautiful," I said. "I'm really impressed. But Ash, how does it solve the problem?"

"Ned wants me to collaborate with him on a song cycle. This is the first song. And Ms. Wilson agreed! I get to go to Forefield every week to work on it. And you can write the lyrics, so you can come too."

"A song cycle! What's a song cycle?"

"Oh, you know—a bunch of songs. If it weren't Forefield, we could just start a band, but this way it's all fancy and official and everything. They're calling it community outreach. It's supposed to improve Forefield's relations with the town if they include Byz High students in some of their programs. Anyway, the point is, we get to work with Ned on writing songs, and we get to go on seeing the guys. Isn't that crisp?"

I heard very little of what my teachers said that day. I lived in reverie. Mr. Klamp said, "Julie, snap out of it" twice, then gave up on me. Ms. Nettleton asked me to read aloud, and I did, but I have no idea what scene I read, even though it was from *Pride and Prejudice*; I didn't hear a word I was saying. Instead, I relived the night before. How much of it I had slept through! How much I had wasted! What did it mean?

⁓

On the way to Forefield, my heart beat harder than it had since the first day of rehearsals. My eyes found Parr as soon as I arrived. He stood in the back but faced the doors, as if he were waiting for me. He looked right at me and smiled. I met his eyes as long as I could, then looked down, blushing. The intensity was too much for me.

The theater was buzzing, as if in sympathy with my heart. A group of actors greeted us excitedly. "Have you guys heard?" said Emma. "Do you know about the disaster?"

"What disaster?" said Ashleigh.

"The sets. Mr. Hatchek got fired. The sets aren't even half done, and nobody can find his plans," said Ravi.

"Why'd he get fired?" I asked.

Chris was lounging a little apart, as if he considered himself above the conversation, but I noticed he still managed to hear what we were saying. "An unspeakable scandal," he said nonchalantly, with, however, a trace of satisfaction.

"What are you talking about? What does *that* mean?"

"Nobody knows," he answered. "Except the administration, presumably. Everybody's speculating. The second formers think he embezzled the art supply fund, and that's why you can't ever find any charcoal."

"Whatever it is, there's no art for the fourth form until they find a new teacher," said Ravi.

"But what about the sets? Opening night's practically next week," cried Ashleigh.

"We'll have to go minimalist," said Ravi. "Empty stage, no curtain, create the sets with sheer acting and the imagination of the audience."

"Or the new teacher could wrestle them into shape, if the school can find one," said Parr, who was somehow standing at my elbow. How had he gotten there? My heart pounded at the sound of his voice. I leaned closer to him; I couldn't help it. So much for easy restraint. Our arms touched.

"Give it a rest, guys, okay?" said Dean Hanson, breaking into our circle. "There's no unspeakable scandal. But we *are* looking for a new art teacher."

"So will we have new sets, or will we finish the old ones?" asked Emma.

"That's for the new teacher to decide, assuming we complete

our search this week. Don't count on it, though. It's not easy to find someone qualified this late in the year."

"Jules—what about your mother?" said Ashleigh suddenly.

"Who—Mom?" I asked, like an idiot.

"Why not? She has an art degree, doesn't she?"

"That's true. She has an MFA. She did a lot of teaching before she married my father."

"Is that so, Julie? Well, tell her to send me her resume. As soon as possible," said the dean. "Now, shouldn't we all get practicing?"

⤫

That Saturday I went with Seth to a reading at the bookstore in town. I had agreed to go under the impression that other people from our magazine would be there, but the only one I saw was Ms. Nettleton. The author, a small, nervous person with a huge head and tiny hands, read a chapter from a novel in which the narrator's mother, dying of cancer, recalls in detail her passionate love affair with a wounded soldier in the French Resistance during World War II. Seth listened with rapt interest, leaning slightly toward me in his folding chair. Did he think the reading would put me in the mood?

As the story rambled from the narrator's mother's bedroom into a description of the French countryside, my mind began to wander to recent events in my own bedroom, and then to the stage at Forefield. I realized with a start that I'd left my copy of my *Insomnia* script, with all my notes in it, on top of the piano where Ned had been using it to rehearse. I had promised to go over Ned's newest changes with Ashleigh—and unless Ned had remembered them and written them down on his script after rehearsal, I had the only copy.

Could I get Seth to drive me to Forefield and pick it up? But what if we ran into someone I knew? No, I would just have to apologize to Ashleigh and wait until next week.

After the reading, I made Seth drop me off at the Lius' instead of at my father's, so Dad and Amy wouldn't have a chance to invite him to dinner again.

"Hot date?" asked Samantha as he drove away.

I made a face. "No, thank God. A book reading, and Ms. Nettleton was there."

"You could let him know you don't like him, you know."

"I know. But he's a decent guy, and I don't want to hurt his feelings."

Sam rolled her eyes. "Well, you're going to be mad when you see who you just missed."

"What do you mean?"

"You had a visitor. Ask your father."

Dad looked up when I came in. "Was that Seth's car? Why didn't you invite him in?"

"He had to get back."

"Too bad, he could have stayed to dinner. Oh, before I forget, a friend of yours came by looking for you. Grant, or something like that? I told him you were out with your boyfriend, so he gave me this for you. He said you left it at school." Dad handed me my script.

My first impulse was to e-mail Parr and deny everything. But what would I say? "Dad's wrong, Seth isn't my boyfriend, it's *you* I like, but so does Ashleigh and therefore my lips are forever sealed"? I had to content myself with kicking the fluffy pillows Amy had made for my new bed and tearing the flier from the reading into a thousand pieces.

༄

My mother quit her job at the Nick-Nack Barn and started at Forefield two days later. She went whistling around the house, mostly songs from the play. I was glad to see her happy again.

Because there was so little time left before *Insomnia* opened, she scrapped Mr. Hatchek's elaborate designs and replaced them with simple colored backdrops—slate gray and white for the lab, institutional yellow for the classroom, leaf green for the magical forest. She worked with the fourth-form painting squad as well as Mark, the lighting designer, and his team of techies to create an atmosphere of enchantment using colored scrims—screens that could look opaque or transparent, depending on how the light hit them. I may be biased, but I thought her designs were much more effective than Mr. Hatchek's fussy backdrops.

And I wasn't the only one who approved. Everyone in the production liked Mom, especially little Alcott Fish, who developed a crush on her that made him turn pink and squeak whenever she was nearby. Ashleigh and I laughed about it privately, but we were careful never to let him see that we'd noticed.

There was one disadvantage to having Mom around, though: no more hanging out with the guys while we waited to be picked up. Mom drove us home as soon as rehearsal ended. I hardly ever got a chance to talk to Parr, and never in private. Not that he seemed eager to talk to me now.

In a whirl of impersonal activity, I watched what I feared might be my last precious hours in his company drain away.

That Tuesday, my stepmother arrived a little earlier than usual to pick me up. She and my mother exchanged words of chilly politeness.

"What was Helen doing there?" asked Amy as we drove away. "Didn't she remember it was Tuesday?"

I explained that Mom had a job at Forefield.

"How nice. I was wondering when she was going to get around to getting a real job. I hope she's planning to tell your father soon. I think their settlement requires her to inform him within sixty days of any change in income," said Amy.

"Of course she is. This is only her third day working there. Has she ever tried to cheat you out of anything that's yours?"

"Hmp," said the Irresistible.

We drove the rest of the way in silence.

After dinner, my father cleared his throat. "Julie, now that you have a boyfriend, there's something Amy and I have to talk to you about," he said. "I know Seth is a trustworthy, reliable young man, and I hope that we've taught you some responsibility over the years. And of course, you're still very young; if we've done our jobs right, it will be a long time before you need to use this knowledge. However, I feel that it's my duty as a physician and a parent—that is, *our* duty as *parents*—" (here he gave Amy a saccharine smile, which she returned) "—to make sure you understand—," etc., etc., etc.

It was—can you believe it?—the Birth Control Talk.

The fourth one, chronologically speaking: Mom had given me the Talk a few years before, when I first got my period; and it had been repeated two consecutive years in Health and Hygiene, the second time with props, including a banana. Mom kept a you'd-better-not-need-these-but-just-in-case-you-do box of condoms in what I thought of as the Embarrassing Corner of the bathroom, updating them when they passed their expiration dates. (I checked.)

Hearing Seth's name coupled with the subject of the Talk

made it doubly disgusting. I begged the floor to open and swallow me, as I had done so often during this distressful year. However, it had never yet obeyed. Why should it start now?

∽

In no time at all, the day of the dress rehearsal arrived. I woke hours early and couldn't get back to sleep. Just one more day, and I would be singing in public.

I felt a horrible foreboding, but I dismissed it as stage fright. I slipped on my lucky thumb ring.

The first hint that something really was wrong came in homeroom. Yolanda sat in uncharacteristic silence, brushing tears away with her tapered fingers.

"Landa," I said hesitantly (since she seemed almost quiet enough to be Yvette), "what's the matter?"

She gave a little yelp and began to cry audibly.

I patted her back. "What is it? What's wrong?"

"Mom caught Yvette being me."

This was serious indeed. In the Gerard household, masquerading as one's sister was a grounding offense.

"Oh, no! How long are you down for this time?"

"Two whole weeks—both of us! We'll miss the play!"

Yvette confirmed the news at lunchtime. "I told you we should have switched the nail polish too," she said bitterly.

Yolanda started crying again. "Mom never noticed before," she gulped.

"That's 'cause you never wore green before."

What would Benjo do? I shuddered to think, but there was no warning him. Forefield boys were forbidden to use cell phones, except during certain evening and weekend hours.

Ashleigh broke the news as soon as we arrived. It took Benjo a while to understand, since he hadn't even known about Yvette's existence, much less her role in his production. As the news sank in, his face grew taut. I watched him pull himself together. He stood up straighter.

"Is there anything we can do to convince Yolanda's parents to change their minds?" he asked.

"Maybe if Ms. Wilson or the dean or somebody goes and talks to them?" said Ashleigh.

"Maybe my mom," I suggested. "She's friendly with Mrs. Gerard."

Benjo sent a second former to find the adults in question.

"Well, there's nothing else we can do about it today," he said. "Julie, you'll have to take over Tanya for now."

"What?" I gasped.

"You play Tanya. You know the part, don't you? You helped them rehearse. I thought you understood—you're the understudy."

"But my part—who'll play Headmistress Lytle?"

"Ned can do it."

"Uh, Benjo?" said Ashleigh. "Ned's a guy. He's a *bass*."

"Well, I know *that*. He'll have to be Head*master* Lytle. One thing's for sure, he knows the part. He'd better—he wrote it. Okay, guys, help me get the cast together so I can make the announcement."

Hard as this may be to believe, it wasn't until Parr said, "So Julia's going to be Tanya?" that I realized what my new part meant.

Chapter 20

I dreamed about kissing Parr. Asleep in my bed, awake in my bed, in that limbo between waking and sleeping that's known as tenth-grade European history, I dreamed about it. But I never dreamed that our first kiss would take place onstage, in front of the entire production of *Midwinter Insomnia*, including my mother.

Although this was the dress rehearsal, there was clearly no way to make the twins' Tanya costume fit me. The clothes I had put on that morning—jeans and a sweater over a long-sleeved, scoop-necked T-shirt—would have to do.

I stood in Tanya's position, twirling my thumb ring on my upstage hand and looking out over a sea of furrowed brows. Concern shone from every eye in the audience, which included everyone in the production not actually onstage. I watched them worry: Would I remember my lines? Would my voice carry? Would I ruin the production they all had worked so hard on?

Gratifyingly, though, after a few minutes the brows began to clear. I was indeed going to remember the lines, my watchers decided one by one. My acting might not be as nuanced as the twins', my singing voice nowhere near as strong, but at least I wasn't going to totally flub it. My mother smiled encouragement at me. Part of me began to relax.

At the same time, though, the rest of me—the better part—began to clench up. For as I stormed at Parr, ordered Alcott Fish around, fell under the spell of the tainted drinking fountain, and fawned over Kevin Rodriguez in his Butthead costume, I knew that the moment I had so often dreamed of was about to arrive, in the most humiliating form imaginable. I would be kissing Parr—Parr, who had been avoiding talking to me, even looking at me—and I'd be doing it in front of an audience. My throat went dry. My voice dropped to a whisper, and Benjo had to say, "Speak up, Julie! Let's take it again from 'Do you admit you were a jerk?' "

Then there was no postponing it. As Owen, Parr admitted the error of his ways. As Tanya, I forgave him. He drew me close—and kissed me.

❧

Was it like kissing Zach? Only the way the merry-go-round is like the Cyclone at Astroland. Only the way sliding down the hill behind the elementary school on your mother's roasting pan is like skiing down Mont Blanc.

I was glad I had kissed Zach. Because of that experience, I didn't flub the kiss onstage any more than I flubbed my lines. I met Parr's lips head-on, without slipping or crashing, and the outside world went dim.

When it was over—rather quickly, I think, because I didn't hear any hooting from the audience, and they *must* have hooted if the kiss had really lasted as long as it seemed to me—I looked up at Parr. His eyes were opaque, abandoned. He looked as overthrown as I felt. Upstage, out of sight of the crowd, he crushed my left hand in his right. I heard a crack and felt my onyx ring snap in two and fall from my thumb.

We stood that way for only an instant; then Alcott Fish entered downstage right, Parr spoke his next line, and the rehearsal swept on to its finale. I spoke and sang mechanically, weak as a kitten.

Afterward, the entire cast and crew gathered around to congratulate me. I was their heroine. I had saved the day, and could now be counted on to save tomorrow too. I looked around for Parr, but it was too public to ask him anything or to tell him anything.

"Come on, girls, get your coats," said Mom. "We'd better get going if I'm going to have time to tackle Marie Gerard before bedtime."

And that was it. Parr and I parted without a word or a touch. Until tomorrow, that is—and tomorrow's kiss.

ﾟﾟﾟ

But it didn't work out that way. Mom's mission was successful. Mrs. Gerard agreed to extend the twins' sentence a week in exchange for their limited release over the next two days.

"How did you do it?" I asked.

"I explained the situation. Marie's a reasonable person," she said.

I gave her a doubtful look. Reasonable or not, Mrs. Gerard had never before reversed a punishment, to my knowledge anyway.

"Oh, all right. I threw myself on her charity. I told her that I was on trial for a job at the school, and that if I managed to get the girls back in the play, it would impress the dean and maybe land me the job."

"Very clever, Mom! That's worthy of Samantha Liu!"

"Yes, and it has the advantage of being true."

With no clear prospect of another kiss from Parr, then, I dwelled on today's. What did it mean? I had watched Parr kiss one twin or another dozens of times apiece, but this kiss seemed different. I had never before seen that look in his eyes— drowned, burning, transformed. Even though he'd hardly spoken to me since my father's horrible remark about Seth, he'd kissed me as if he meant it. I thought it must mean something.

I thought it must mean he liked me.

But Ashleigh! Ashleigh. Even if he *did* like me, that didn't release me from my obligation to my best friend. As long as *she* liked *him*, my hands were tied.

Had Ashleigh noticed anything strange? Apparently not. "You were wow, Jules!" she cried, bursting through the front door after dinner. "I told you you could do it! Did your mom get Mrs. Gerard to relent? She did? Really? Too bad! I mean, crisp for Yv and Yo, of course, but too bad for you, you were so incredible as Tanya! And Ned was great too. I don't see why he didn't want a part in the first place, he has a loudly crisp voice. I loved you in your scenes with Kevin, you were both so, so funny, and you were great with Parr too. You're a natural. Next time you'll get a bigger part. No question! You just needed the practice. I bet you could even get into a Byz production now, if it wasn't such a popularity contest with Michelle Jeffries and all those people." Et cetera. Evidently the struggle going on within me had made no impression on my friend.

⤳

After the excitement of the dress rehearsal, opening night seemed almost tame. I relaxed into my old role of Headmistress Lytle with a calm and control that surprised me, and I handed over Tanya's part to Yvette with relief. Yolanda had agreed that after all her sister's hard work and risky pretending, it was only fair for Yvette to go first.

Our parents came to opening night—the Rossis sat in the front row, clapping wildly at pretty much everything—but mostly the audience was a sea of boys in blazers. Ravi missed the line he always missed; he smiled his beguiling smile, and the audience forgave him with a laugh. Ashleigh sang loud and clear, Alcott sweet and true. We all hit our high notes and our low notes. The ensemble numbers went smoothly, nobody tripping or crashing. Numb with adrenaline, I watched from the wings as Parr kissed Yvette. I even enjoyed my bow and the applause that came with it. How far I had come from the terror of the audition so many months ago!

The cast party afterward didn't last very long, since the performance was only a small part of the packed Founder's Day schedule. Chris had managed to smuggle in a fifth of vodka, but Mr. Barnaby found it in the prop room and confiscated it with grim warnings before Chris could use it to spike the hot chocolate, punch, and other virtuous beverages provided by the school. Mr. Barnaby, Ms. Wilson, Benjo, and Ned all made speeches. Everyone hugged or hit one another on the back.

I saw Parr across the room. He looked away quickly. Was he not going to say anything, even tonight? I felt I couldn't bear it. Everyone was happy, everyone was hugging. Even if he *was* Ashleigh's crush, even if he didn't seem to want to talk to me anymore, at least this one night nobody would think it was strange if I . . . I walked across the room and put my arms around him.

"Congratulations, Grandison, you were great," I said, managing to keep my voice steady.

He hugged me back, hard. "Julia!" he said. "You too—last night, especially." He looked at me at last, his eyes close enough to burn me with their gas-blue flames, and I thought . . . But then the twins and Emma came over to deliver their own hugs, and he let me go. The party ended soon afterward.

The second and final performance the next day was much the same as the first, but with Yolanda's sunnier Tanya and an older audience, Old Boys (alumni) instead of current students.

After our curtain calls, Dean Hanson and the headmaster took over to make what amounted to a fund-raising pitch. Ned stayed onstage as the Live Performance Scholar, an example of the great things that resulted when Old Boys opened their checkbooks. But Parr slipped away and found me backstage where I was waiting for Ashleigh. "Here—these are for you," he said. He handed me a bunch of flowers wrapped in blank newsprint.

Ashleigh came up, carrying an armload of bundled costumes and props. "There you are," she said. "I don't think we can wait for Ned—he said it would take another hour. We better get going. Your mom'll be waiting."

"I'll walk you," said Parr.

On the way out of the theater, a woman in the audience stopped him. They had the same eyes. "Snip, that was wonderful," she said.

"Thanks, Mom. But not in public, remember?"

"Oh—right—sorry, Snip, I forgot."

"*Mother!* Matricide!"

"Sorry, sorry, I mean Grandison."

"That's better. Mom, this is Ashleigh Rossi and Julia Lefkowitz. My mother, Susan Parr. I'll be right back, Mom, I'm just going to see Julia and Ashleigh out."

"It's nice to meet you, girls. Don't be too long, Sn— Grandison, your father's trapped in there with the headmaster."

" 'Snip'?" I asked as we walked down the drive.

"It's short for Parsnip, I'm sorry to say. She's not supposed to call me that in public. I wish she hadn't. I love her, and it'll pain me to kill her."

"Snip is better than Junior," said Ashleigh.

"It's better than Parsley or Parboiled. Or Sley or Boiled," I suggested.

"Don't," said Parr. "It would pain me even more to kill *you*."

"Tridge," I said. "Terre. Ticipation. Kinglot. Liament."

"Enough! Mercy!"

"All right, Typooper." I was giddy with relief that we seemed to be on speaking terms again. We approached the end of the drive.

"When will I see you again?" asked Parr. "You're coming to the Spring Frolic, aren't you? I'll send you tickets. But it's not until April."

"Didn't Ned tell you?" said Ashleigh. "We're collaborating on a song cycle. Ms. Wilson said we could—it counts as community outreach. We meet on Thursday afternoons, when the music studio is free."

"Oh, Ash! You didn't say it was Thursdays! I can't make it then," I said. "That's when *Sailing* meets."

"I didn't know you sailed," said Parr. "So do I—my father's obsessed with sailing. Maybe I'll go out for it in the spring. We could meet on the river."

"Not sailing boats—*Sailing to Byzantium*, our literary magazine," I explained.

Parr stiffened. "Oh, I see," he said.

Oh, no! He was clearly thinking of Seth. Had I ruined everything? Was there anything I could say? "I wish I could quit—I would, but Dad would kill me, especially now that *Insomnia's* over and I don't have any other extracurriculars," I said.

Parr relaxed slightly. "Well, I'm sure I'll think of something," he said. "Ski break isn't that far off, anyway."

"Ski break? What's that?" said Ashleigh.

"You know—mid-February vacation—Presidents' Day and all that. Don't you get off for it?" We shook our heads. "Well, we do," said Parr. "My parents like to go to Vermont, but I think this would be a good year to stay at our place in Steeplecliff instead."

We reached the gate and my mother's car and said our good-byes.

When Ashleigh deposited her armload of props and costumes in the backseat, I saw she was also carrying a bunch of flowers in newsprint. Hers were tulips; she looked at mine, which were something tall and lilylike. "Oh, Ned gave you flowers too!" she said.

"These are from Parr."

"Yeah, Ned told me he stole them from the Conservatory. Turkeyface almost caught him," she said proudly. "It's just like him to share them with Parr."

As we drove away, I saw Parr standing by the gate, looking after us until we turned the corner of the drive.

Chapter 21

A Nonstatic Screen Wipe ⌒ Ashleigh's new Craze.

And that was it. No more *Midwinter Insomnia*. No more Parr. The weeks stretched out before me, blank and numb.

Ashleigh, lucky thing, began her musical collaboration at Forefield that Thursday, while I stayed at school for the *Sailing* meeting.

"Slim pickings here," said our editor, Eleanor, waving a few pages, the only submissions so far. "Come on, guys, beat the bushes. Pound the pavement—pester the talent. Get your ear in gear. What's the matter, doesn't *anyone* have a masterpiece in a drawer somewhere? Maggie? Andrew? Julie? What's wrong with you! Come on, Julie, I know you have something squirreled away. Of course you do, you always have ink up and down your arms."

"Don't be shy, Julie," said Seth. "What about that sonnet you said you were writing?"

I denied it. Any expression I might have given to my feelings was too private, too sacred for those eyes.

Since my mother was still at work, Seth drove me home after the meeting. "Don't you want to show me your sonnet?" he coaxed, parking in front of my house. He was clearly angling to be invited in. "I could help you make the rhyme and meter work before you submit it to the board, if that's what you're nervous about. I bet it won't be too hard to fix it."

"There is no sonnet! Leave it alone, okay?" I said irritably, getting out of the car.

"All right! Sorry. I didn't realize you'd be so touchy," said Seth. "You don't have to be, you know—you're really a pretty good writer."

"Yeah, thanks, see you tomorrow," I said, shutting the door hard and going into the house quickly.

I went upstairs and e-mailed Parr. I tried not to, but I couldn't help it.

Thanks again for the beautiful flowers. They've just finished opening. I have them on my desk, where I can see them whenever I look up. Did Ned really steal them from the conservatory, like Ashleigh says?

Parr wrote back at once:

Dear Julia,
Do you think I would let someone else commit my crimes for me? I stole every one of those amaryllises with my own hands.
I miss you.
CGP

He missed me! The words made my inky arms tingle, and I confess I kissed the screen where they appeared. Did he mean it? Did he miss me as much as I missed him? But what good would all the missing in the world do, when he was *there* and I was *here* and Ashleigh lay between us? Almost screaming with frustration, I got a nonstatic wipe out of my desk drawer and cleaned the mark of my lips off the screen.

〜

When Seth drove me home again a week later, Ashleigh was waiting for me on her porch, wrapped in the big down throw from the Rossis' couch. "There you are, Julie," she said, hurrying down the steps. The corner of the throw trailed in the dry grass. "I need to talk to you."

Seth set his jaw sourly. By now he must hate Ashleigh as much as my stepmother did, but I was grateful to have a chaperone for the dangerous end of the drive, the most likely moment for a guy to lunge. I knew he wouldn't do anything with Ashleigh hovering over us. He let me out and drove off at once.

"Thanks, Ash," I said after he was gone. "I keep being afraid he's going to kiss me good-bye. What's up?"

She looked grave and uncomfortable. "It's cold out here. Let's go up to my room," she said.

I followed her upstairs and sat down on her bed. She sat on her desk chair, fidgeting, weirdly quiet.

"What's wrong?" I asked. "Why are you acting all weird?"

"Jules, I . . ." She stopped, took a deep breath, and started again. "Julie, is it really true . . ." She trailed off.

"What? Is what really true?"

"Is it true that—is it true what you're always saying about Ned?"

"What? Ash, tell me what's wrong. I don't understand what you're talking about. What am I always saying about Ned?" She opened and closed her mouth a few times, but didn't manage to answer. "What do you mean?" I said. "I'm not the one who talks about Ned all the time—you are. I don't know why you want to believe I like him, but I don't. I mean, he's a nice guy and every-thing, but I just don't *like* him."

"That! That's what I mean," said Ashleigh. "Is it really true? You're not just saying that?"

"What, that I don't like him? *Yes*, it's really true. Why would I be just saying that? I keep telling you it's true! I keep telling you over and over! Why don't you want to believe it?"

"You're sure?"

"YES, I'M SURE! Why are you going on about this?"

"Because—" Ashleigh took a deep breath. "I . . . He . . . We . . ."

My heart began to pound before I knew why. Then I knew why. "Ash! *You* like him! Is *that* it?"

She gave a strangled nod.

I had never before seen her speechless like this. I felt like whooping. I threw my arms around her. "Ash! You're perfect for each other!"

"You don't mind, then?"

"*Mind*? Why would I mind? That my best friend likes a re-ally nice guy? And he likes you too, right? It's so obvious! The flowers! The music! Why didn't I see it? He does, doesn't he?"

She nodded. "I think so," she said. "At least—he kissed me."

"He *kissed* you? What? When? Tell me!"

It had happened in the soundproofed rehearsal room. "When you spend a lot of time with someone, and you realize all the things you have in common, like music and liking to do fun things like playing little tricks on people and trying out differ-ent instruments and really talking about stuff, and there we were sitting on the same piano bench in complete privacy because nobody could hear us, and oh, Julie! He's so wonderful! He has the most beautiful voice! And his hands are so strong from playing the piano and his left hand has these wonderful calluses from the cello. Don't you love the cello? It has that soulful, sexy sound— just like Ned's voice. Kissing him is absolutely nothing like kissing Ravi. He was a little shy, so I kissed him first, but he said afterward that he was about to kiss me a split second later."

Once they realized how they felt, said Ashleigh, the only thing that stood in their way was Ashleigh's loyal determination not to destroy what she thought, generous girl, was my happiness. She still had trouble believing that I was telling the truth— she had trouble believing that anyone could know Ned and not love him as she did. I had to reassure her over and over.

I considered admitting that there was Someone Else for me too, but I held off. I knew how much trouble she would have turning her focus from the subject that engrossed her—but once she did, there would be no holding her back. My tender feelings weren't yet ready for the full force of Ashleigh. Besides, I didn't want to spoil her moment.

For the rest of the evening she poured out her joy. I soon realized that her new attachment represented not merely a change of love interest, but a full-out craze change. How had I missed it? The signs had all been there: her relenting about whether to expose the lower limbs, the intensity of her interest in *Midwinter Insomnia*. Her parents had noticed her new enthusiasm for Broadway long before I did—hence the tickets to *Fascination!* And our visit to Parr's town house, I now realized, had been for Ned's sake, not Parr's.

"What about Parr?" I asked at length, my heart beating hard.

"What about him?"

"You said you liked him back in October—remember? You seemed pretty serious about it."

"Oh—yes—well, I thought I did, but that was before I really understood what Love was. You were right after all when you thought Ned was Darcy! Nothing against Parr, he's a really nice guy, but he's no Ned. He just doesn't have the same fire—the talent—the intensity—the inventive good humor—the *life*. You know what I mean?"

Smiling to myself, I said I could see how she would think so.

Chapter 22

The B-word ∽ Seth vanquished ∽ a Ring ∽
my Sixth Kiss ∽ an Acrostic.

I fell asleep that night in a dazzle of happiness. Honor no longer stood between me and my heart's desire.

I awoke the next day, however, to a gray, spitting drizzle and the realization that, although everything had changed, nothing had changed. True, I was free to love Parr. But I wasn't free to see him.

Also, I remembered, I had promised in a weak moment to hang out at the Java Jail with Seth that afternoon after school. When I made the promise, it had seemed like ages in the future, too far away to matter; but now the time had arrived. I saw myself sinking slowly into the swamp of Seth's expectations, while the golden sail of my love twinkled out of sight over the horizon.

rescue me ash, I text-messaged my friend. *meeting seth @java j this aftnn. be there pls. pls pls pls. need you. jl*

you shd dump him already. quit messing around. its too imptnt. dont worry tho ill be there. ash, she TM'ed back.

And she was. "Jules! Seth! Come sit over here," she shrieked from the back, patting two seats at her table. I headed stubbornly in her direction, with Seth dragging behind and trying to draw me off to other tables.

Once we had sat down, Ashleigh pounced on Seth. "As a literary person, what qualities would you say it's important to look for in poetry if you want to set it to music?" she asked him.

It was the perfect question, at once flattering and absorbing, and even useful (at least to Ashleigh). After a few increasingly feeble attempts to get away, Seth warmed to the subject. He almost seemed to forget his irritation at Ashleigh and his resentful yearning for me. He turned his face and shoulders toward her, leaving me behind at his elbow. I was never more grateful to Ash.

Their conversation left my mind free to wander. It headed off in the usual direction—toward Parr.

And then, as if I had summoned him, there he was. He was weaving his way through the crowded coffee bar in front of Zach Liu.

"Here you go, Stringbean, a late birthday present," said Zach with a smirk, pushing Parr forward.

"Zach! Parr! Hey, have a seat," cried Ashleigh, pushing out a chair. Zach sat down next to her. "Seth, you know Zach Liu, don't you?" said Ashleigh. She gave Parr a wink and a kick as she continued with the shocking words, "And have you met Grandison Parr, Julie's boyfriend?"

"Your boyfriend!" exclaimed Seth.

I felt the blood drain to my feet. I looked at Parr with terrified inquiry. He smiled back, a sweet, wicked smile, full of mischief and hope. I took a breath and decided to go with it. "Yes," I said, "my boyfriend, Grandison. I think you guys met before, right?"

"Hello, *sweetie*," said Parr, coming over to sit next to me.

"I didn't realize you were going out," said Seth stiffly.

"Oh, we weren't—then, I mean," I said. "That is, we . . ."

Zach looked as if he might burst out laughing at any moment.

"We were just talking about what makes a poem a true lyric," said Ashleigh quickly, drawing the attention to a safer corner of the table. "Seth says it's the meter and the quality of the assonance and alliteration, but what do you think, Parr? Parr wrote all the lyrics for *Insomnia*. He's amazing. That's what brought him and Julie together. She's really sensitive to poetry," she babbled.

I felt the old sensation, familiar from years of Ashleigh: mortal embarrassment. I turned my face away. Parr put his arm around my shoulder. "Are you all right, *sweetie*?" he said.

"She'll be fine, now that you're here," said Ashleigh. I straightened back up and kicked her under the table.

Seth cleared his throat. He looked pale. I felt bad for him. "Well, I'd better be going," he said, standing up. "Lots of homework this weekend."

"Oh, must you? Well, nice to meet you," said Zach.

"Bye, Seth, see you Monday," I said.

"Tuesday," said Ashleigh. "Long weekend."

"Right. Tuesday."

Seth made a pained little bowlike gesture and left.

"Ashleigh!" I said. "That was so embarrassing. And kind of mean."

"Why? You've been complaining for weeks about how you need help getting rid of him."

"Have you?" said Parr.

"Yes, she has," said Ashleigh. "You know it's meaner to let him keep hanging around when you don't actually like him. Now I won't have to chaperone you all the time."

Something in that sentence made Zach look at his watch. "Ope! Gotta go. Come on, Ashcan, I'll give you a ride home," he said.

"Thanks, Zach, that's okay, you don't have to," began Ashleigh.

"Don't be an idiot—come on—there's something my sister needs you to do," said Zach, taking her firmly by the shoulder.

"What? Oh. Oh! Right, that thing for Sam," said Ashleigh, grabbing her coat with one hand as Zach propelled her to the door. "Later, guys."

Then I was all by myself in the crowded coffee bar with Charles Grandison Parr. He grinned at me, took my hand, and said, "*Sweetie!* Alone at last!"

❧

Maybe it was all a big joke, but I noticed his hand was as cold as ice.

Did it tremble a little? Mine certainly did.

"Ashleigh can be so embarrassing," I said. "Sorry! Or, I guess, I mean, thanks."

"Don't mention it. I'm honored that I could be of use to you. Especially to get rid of guys who pester you. Anytime you find a guy troublesome, please feel free to tell him I'm your boyfriend."

"You mean it?" I said.

"You know I do. If you think it'll help, I'll even come by and threaten him with my epee—my dueling sword. Speaking of getting rid of guys," he added, "are you done with your coffee? Would you like to walk down to the river? I see some of the guys from the fencing team heading this way, and I don't particularly want to hang out with them. I get to see them all the time. I never get to see *you*."

"Sure," I said.

Parr left a tip on the table and helped me into my coat. Nobody had done that since I was a little girl; I fumbled around for the sleeves a bit before he found my arms and lifted the coat around my shoulders.

It was a warm afternoon for February, the earliest edge of spring. The rain had stopped, leaving a breath of moisture in the air. We walked the six blocks to the train tracks in silence, smelling the river just beyond, and crossed the tracks by the underpass, with its buzzing lights and loud echoes. The other side seemed quiet by contrast, hushed with the soft, deep slipping of the river.

"Let's see if anyone's in the band shell," said Parr.

No one was. Everyone else, apparently, remembered it was February.

We sat down on one of the wooden benches overlooking the river; the band shell kept the worst of the wind off.

"What are you doing out of school, anyway?" I asked.

"Ski break, remember? I'm staying with my folks in Steeplecliff. Actually, I was looking for you. I wanted to give you something." He took a little box out of his pocket and handed it to me.

"What is it?" I said. I had to take my gloves off to open the box. My hands trembled. I held it carefully, trying not to drop it. Inside was a ring: one side solid silver, the other side silver encasing something black.

"Does it still fit?" asked Parr. "Try it on. I was worried I might have made it too small—I had to add a strip of silver underneath the onyx. If it doesn't fit, give it back. I can make it bigger."

"You *made* this?"

He nodded.

The ring was too big for my fingers, but it fit my left thumb perfectly. I looked at it more closely. "Wait," I said. "Don't tell me it's my onyx ring! The one that got broken?"

"I felt terrible about breaking it," he said. "I thought I should do something."

"You didn't have to . . . You *made* this? But it's so beautiful. Is there *anything* you can't do?"

He laughed. "Well, yes. Tons. Most of the important things. One thing I thought I probably couldn't—but I don't know, I'm starting to think maybe I can. Let's see."

And he kissed me.

How cold his lips were—and then how warm. My sixth kiss—but my first. The blue sky, the blue river, his blue drowned look, our breath steaming together into one cloud. My cold fingers—his cold neck, warm under his scarf. I touched his dimple. We kissed again.

"I take it back," he said, his voice rough. "You're right. There's nothing I can't do." He took off my hat and kissed my forehead, my cheekbones, the edges of my face next to my eyes. "I wanted to do that so badly," he said. "Especially that night."

"Why didn't you?" I said.

"Why didn't I? What do you take me for—barge into a girl's room in the middle of the night and start kissing her? And I wasn't sure you even liked me."

"But I was being so obvious—joining the play and hanging around you all the time helping you rehearse."

I was trembling. He hugged me to him and put his chin on top of my head. I heard his voice through my bones. My heart pounded and pounded.

"You call that obvious?" he said. "You never talked to me unless I said something first. And then there was that Seth person; everyone kept saying he was your boyfriend. I almost gave up."

"Oh, God, Seth—he was so awful, I wanted to die. But I thought you had a girlfriend too. Some friend of Samantha Liu's saw you dancing with a tall blonde at the Columbus dance. She said it was your girlfriend."

He drew back and looked at me. "What? You're kidding, right?"

"No, that's what Sam said."

He laughed. "Well, she was almost right. I *was* dancing with an enchanting blonde, but she wasn't my girlfriend—not then, anyway. Do you really not know who it was?"

I felt as if I were standing inches from a sheer cliff, balanced over sharp rocks of jealousy. I hid my face against him again. "Sam's friend thought it was Kayla somebody?" I mumbled into his coat.

"No, silly! It was *you*! You really didn't know? There I was making a gigantic fool of myself, mooning around your house and writing you poetry, and I couldn't even tell if you had read it. That was the first thing that made me hope: seeing you had my sonnet up on your bulletin board. But you never said anything about it."

"But I wasn't sure you wrote the sonnet for *me*. I thought it was for Ashleigh."

"For Ashleigh!" He drew back again and looked at me. "But it had your name in it!"

"You mean *July*? 'Zero degrees down here, July above?' That's what Ashleigh said, but I didn't believe her."

"No, I mean your name! Well, July too—I put it in for the echo—but I'm talking about your actual name, Julia Lefkowitz.

Going down the side, the first letters of the lines. It's an acrostic—fourteen letters, fourteen lines. You mean you didn't even notice? Wow, I feel silly."

Not as silly as I felt. My own name! Right there in the sonnet that the Person of My Heart wrote for me—and I didn't even see it.

"Okay, I'm a marshmallow brain," I said. "Do you hate me now?"

The answer took a while and was more absorbing than I could have thought possible. Afterward, I no longer knew how many times I'd been kissed.

Chapter 23

Bliss ⟶ Farewell.

*T*hen followed ten days of unprecedented bliss. Parr found a way to come to Byzantium almost every day, and although the weather retreated into winter again, we barely noticed the cold. We held hands through the thriller and the romantic comedy at the Cinepalace, without noticing a single explosion or kiss (on-screen, at least). We spent hours talking about books in Andrezo's Diner, the Java Jail's unfashionable rival, where the coffee was hot, the patrons were scruffy, and the booths had high backs.

Ashleigh and Ned, who was staying at Forefield over the vacation, sometimes joined us. When they did, the noise level in the diner tripled.

After Mom's success with the Gerards, Dean Hanson persuaded the headmaster to offer her a contract for the following year. She informed my father immediately by registered mail. Flush with her settled new income, she turned the thermostat up to 68 degrees, and in her happiness she even converted the Treasures storeroom back into a painting studio, as it had been during the early years of my parents' marriage. Parr and I spent an afternoon helping her.

Parr brought me to lunch at his parents' on the second

Saturday of the break. Their house in Steeplecliff had stone walls, low ceilings, and slanted floors; I could tell it was very old.

"So this is what was fascinating Snip in Byzantium all week! I was starting to wonder," said Ms. Parr—or Susan, as she told me to call her—with a familiar flashing smile.

To my great relief, I found that my table manners were not noticeably different from the Parrs'; Charles Grandison Sr.— Chip—even punctuated his points by gesturing with his chicken leg. And to my surprise, he took to me at once, insisting on giving me a tour of the barn out back where he was building a sailboat. "See if you can get Snip to take an interest," he told me. "Half his ancestors were sea captains."

I found Parr's room upstairs delightfully revealing. Although he had clearly cleaned up in my honor, he was just as clearly a natural slob. Books, abandoned bird nests, and bits of fencing equipment lay in loosely squared stacks in the corners. He turned out to be an avid bird-watcher. It was the wrong season for the more exotic migrants, but he regaled me with stories of the loves and rivalries of the local crows.

He had the entire Patrick O'Brian series of naval novels in a heap behind the door and admitted to having read them all— "But don't tell my dad, it would please him too much," he said. He lent me the first one after making me promise to keep it away from Ashleigh for a few weeks. "Let her go on sharing Ned's interests for as long as possible."

I found it hard to drag myself to school during that heavenly period. I particularly resented the Thursday afternoon wasted at *Sailing*. Seth took care to talk to me just as much as ever, as if to prove that there had been nothing particular behind his attentions. But he soon took up with Margaret Barsky, a tall, pretty girl in Ms. Milburn's third-period bio, who had hair the same color as mine. They appeared regularly as a couple at the Cinepalace and the Java Jail. I often caught her looking at me with triumph tinged with dislike. From time to time, too, I caught a glance from Seth so full of some strangled emotion that I regretted ever having allowed him to think—whatever it was he *had* thought.

My father and stepmother mourned Seth's loss as if he had been one of their own dreamed-of babies. Parr, they pointedly let me know, would never replace him in their affections.

When Forefield started up again, Parr and I had to sustain ourselves with e-mail for several weeks. Then we had the happy thought of volunteering at the Byzantium Senior Center at the same time on Tuesday evenings. It was a savvy move for college applications—or at least, that's how I presented it to Dad.

Yvette Gerard, after her *Insomnia* experience, found she liked acting as much as her sister did. With some help behind the scenes from Samantha, the twins and Ashleigh seized control of Byz High's spring musical from the Michelle Jeffries clique. Ash volunteered to compose the music, and after some persuasion, I agreed to write the lyrics.

With all my new activities, time flew by. It's April already. The Forefield Spring Frolic is this Saturday. Parr and Ned gave us our tickets as soon as they were printed, and we look forward to producing them at the first sight of Turkeyface.

Ash has been giggling mysteriously all week, hiding sheets of music whenever I show up at her window. (The tree lost its ice weeks ago, but I have to be careful not to tear the tender young leaves.) I suspect she and Ned may be planning to surprise me with a waltz or a quadrille arrangement of the tune to which

Ashleigh set the poem I wrote so long ago, when Parr seemed to me only a hopeless dream.

So far, Ashleigh's musical craze has held strong, and Parr and I have high hopes that even when it changes, as it inevitably will, her loyalty to those she loves will not allow her to leave Ned behind.

ACKNOWLEDGMENTS

No writer could have a warmer friend or a more generous reader than Anna Christina Büchmann, or a keener, more loving husband than Andrew Nahem, who gave me my best joke and taught me everything I know about happy endings. For their insight, encouragement, and generosity I'm greatly indebted also to Nancy Paulsen, my editor; Irene Skolnick, my agent; and Michael Abrams, Mark Caldwell, Eunice Chan, Stacey D'Erasmo, Lisa Dierbeck, Carol Dweck, John Hart, Elizabeth Judd, Katherine Keenum, Eleanor Liu, Anne Malcolm, Shanti Menon, Christina Milburn, Laura Miller, Laurie Muchnick, James O'Shea, Lisa Randall, Jenna Reback, Maggie Robbins, Andrew Solomon, Cindy Spiegel, Jaime Wolf, and Shenglan Yuan. And for their love, support, intelligence, and humor I'm grateful to my family: my brother, Theodore Shulman; my mother and stepfather, Alix Kates Shulman and Scott York; my father and stepmother, Martin and Beverly Shulman; and all the Nahems, especially my niece Emily and my father-in-law, Sam, who was as beloved as he was bald.

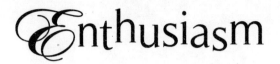
Enthusiasm

READER'S GUIDE

Little-known facts about
Enthusiasm and Jane Austen

• Jane Austen's niece, Anna, wrote a novel called *Enthusiasm*, which she sent to her aunt. Jane had many encouraging things to say, including suggesting that Anna change the title to *Which is the Heroine?*

• The character of Charles Grandison Parr—or Parr for short—was named after Sir Charles Grandison, the hero of Samuel Richardson's 1753 novel of that name and one of Jane Austen's favorite literary characters.

• Jane Austen published her novels anonymously, as was the custom of female writers at the time.

• Like many of Austen's heroines, Jane herself turned down an offer of marriage that would have allowed her to live a more comfortable life and be less dependent on her family. In the end, she never married.

The Life and Legacy of Jane Austen

Jane Austen (1775–1817) lived her entire life in the English countryside with her mother, father, sister, and two brothers. She never married nor ventured far from the confines of her family's home, yet she wrote some of the most enduring novels of her time, including *Pride and Prejudice*, *Sense & Sensibility*, and *Emma*.

When Jane Austen penned her first novel in 1789, little did she know that the stories she acted out in her drawing room with her sister and brothers would affect popular culture hundreds of years later. Dozens of movie adaptations of her novels have been made and continue to be popular, starring actors such as Keira Knightley, Gwyneth Paltrow, Kate Winslet, Colin Firth, and Hugh Grant. Her writing has inspired other books as well, such as *Bridget Jones's Diary*, *The Jane Austen Book Club*, and *Jane Austen's Guide to Dating*.

Discussion Questions

1.   Why do you think Jane Austen and her books have endured as long as they have? Why do Jane Austen's stories translate so well into modern stories?

2.   Have you ever read any of Jane Austen's books? If so, what similarities and differences do you see between Austen's works and *Enthusiasm*?

3.   "There is little more likely to exasperate a person of sense than finding herself tied by affection and habit to an Enthusiast." Do you know/have known an enthusiast? Were you ever one yourself? Although Julie complains about her friend's enthusiasm, what admirable qualities can be found in Ashleigh's exuberance?

4.   If you could produce a movie based on a Jane Austen story, which would you choose and from what angle would you approach it: Comedy or drama? Present day or historical setting?

5.   Have you ever had a crush on the same person as your best friend? If so, what happened?

6.   Throughout the story Julie is careful to point out what a good friend Ashleigh is to her. Unfortunately, Ashleigh's not always a very good listener. At the same time, Julie is keeping secrets from Ashleigh. Could you still say they are great friends? Why or why not?

7.   Class was an important issue for people in Jane Austen's time. In what ways does the issue of class/money come up in *Enthusiasm*?

8.   Do you think Julie handles her relationship with her stepmother well? What could Julie and her stepmother do to improve their relationship?